SUZY'S
SECRET SNOOP
SOCIETY

MARY ANDERSON is the author of over two dozen books for young readers and enjoys writing both comedies and mysteries. She is a native New Yorker and often uses the city as the background for her stories.

Suzy's Secret Snoop Society

MARY ANDERSON

AN AVON CAMELOT BOOK

To DEAN MORTON AND HIS WIFE PAMELA,
*who have helped make the cathedral
a special place*

SUZY'S SECRET SNOOP SOCIETY is an original publication of Avon Books. This work has never before appeared in book form. Greg Wyatt, the sculptor, is a real person. All other characters and all events depicted in *Suzy's Secret Snoop Society* are entirely fictitious.

AVON BOOKS
A division of
The Hearst Corporation
105 Madison Avenue
New York, New York 10016

Copyright © 1991 by Mary Anderson
Published by arrangement with the author
Library of Congress Catalog Card Number: 90-93201
ISBN: 0-380-75917-9
RL: 4.6

First Avon Camelot Printing: January 1991

CAMELOT TRADEMARK REG. U.S. PAT. OFF. AND IN OTHER COUNTRIES, MARCA REGIS-
TRADA, HECHO EN U.S.A.

Printed in the U.S.A.

OPM 10 9 8 7 6 5 4 3 2 1

Chapter One

"Something's wrong," Suzy Pierce told herself. She felt awful. This was her first day at Coleridge Academy, it was already twelve o'clock, and she still hadn't made a friend. "Don't be nervous," she thought, "start mingling."

Suzy strolled through the schoolyard. She smiled at several girls but none of them smiled back. "What's the matter?" she wondered.

As Suzy passed the benches, she noticed her older sister, Sarabeth, playing basketball. "Is Sarabeth having better luck?" she wondered. She decided to play, too. But when Suzy tried getting into a game, a chorus of angry voices started shouting.

"Off base!" they yelled. "Wimp alert! Call out the Pea-Pod-Squad!"

Jesse Leroy was sitting on a bench watching. "You're out of bounds," she explained. "Fifth graders never shoot baskets until the ten-through-twelvers leave. It's tradition."

"I didn't know that," said Suzy defensively.

"Ten-through-twelvers have seniority and like to throw their weight around," said Jesse. She pointed to the teenage boy shouting the loudest. "See that

1

tenth grader? That's my brother, Calvin. He thinks he's the hottest shot here but he's actually an idiot."

Suzy hated being yelled at. "That basketball rule sounds asinine to me."

Jesse wasn't sure what asinine meant. "I bet you like to read a lot."

"Sure, I love books. Don't you?"

"No way. I watch movies instead. Sooner or later, whatever is important in books gets put in a movie."

Suzy was still upset. "How long has Coleridge had that dumb basketball rule?"

"Forever. I told you, it's tradition."

"Well it's not fair," Suzy argued. "That means my sister Sarabeth gets to play before I do and she's rotten at basketball. What sense does that make?"

"Which one is your sister?" asked Jesse.

Suzy pointed to a tall blonde girl. "That's Sarabeth. She's a tenth grader, too."

"She's awfully pretty."

"No she's not, she's a jerk."

"She can't be a bigger jerk than my brother Calvin."

"Wait until you meet her." Suzy sat down on a bench and sighed. "I hope the first day at a new school is the worst, because so far this has been disgusting."

"I figured you were new here," said Jesse. "Where are you from?"

"We used to live in Connecticut until we moved to Manhattan a week ago," Suzy explained. "Everything is so different here in the city. I miss my old school already. And I don't think I fit in. I've noticed kids keep looking at me like I'm weird."

"That's because you're dressed all wrong," said Jesse.

2

Suzy glanced at her new sweater, jeans, and sneakers. "I spent ages dressing this morning."

"Well it's all wrong," Jesse told her. "All your clothes are *new*. Coleridge kids never wear new stuff the first day. Only geekoids do that. New clothes have no style."

"That's great," said Suzy. "The first day and I'm already labeled a dweeb. I'll never make any friends here now."

"Don't get so intense, it's not the end of the world."

"Yes it is," said Suzy. "It's awful not to fit in. It's horrible being the new person and not knowing the rules. And it stinks to be yelled at by twelvers. I wish we'd never moved."

Jesse felt sorry for Suzy. "Stay cool, you're not a total dweeb yet," she assured. Then she stepped on Suzy's sneakers. "See, I dirtied them up for you." Then Jesse scooped up a handful of earth and rubbed it into Suzy's jeans. "Isn't that better? Now you have a lived-in look."

A horrid thought suddenly struck Suzy. "This isn't a trick, is it? Are you playing a dirty joke on me?"

Jesse laughed. "No, honest I'm not."

Suzy wasn't sure. "I think you're trying to make me look ridiculous," she shouted, wiping the dirt from her jeans.

As Suzy hurried back into the school building, Jesse stared after her.

During English class, Jesse forgot all about her exchange with Suzy at lunchtime. She was far too busy drooling over her English teacher. Jesse had a giant crush on Mr. MacPherson. She was dying to impress him with her literary knowledge but she didn't have

3

any. Jesse never managed higher than a C in English.

Mr. MacPherson pushed aside a lock of wavy brown hair. "I hope you're prepared for a challenging year. I've planned a great book report project this term. Each of you will pretend you're a famous character from fiction, then write about yourself. Have fun, be imaginative, enjoy yourselves."

Jesse sighed. She'd love to write a decent book report just once in her life.

At dinner that night, Jesse was still preoccupied.

Calvin flipped sweet peas from his spoon, shooting them in her direction. "Jess is a mess. It's el crusho time again. The Big Mac has turned her brain to musho."

Jesse ignored him as always.

"Did you have a good first day at school?" asked her mother.

"Did you meet any new kids?" asked her father.

"Just one," said Jesse. "Her name is Suzy Pierce."

"That's a coincidence," said Mrs. Leroy. "The Pierce family just moved into this building. Isn't that nice?"

"I don't think so," said Jesse. "Suzy wasn't nice at all. She whined and complained and acted like a dope. And she wore all the wrong clothes. I think she's awfully snooty."

"It sounds like Suzy is scared," said Mrs. Leroy. "I remember I acted like that my first day in junior high."

"Really?" asked Jesse. "Did you really act like a jerk?"

"Absolutely," said Mrs. Leroy. "Of course, I pretended I knew everything, which made me look even

4

dopier. And I was wearing stockings while all the other girls wore socks. I thought everyone would hate me all year just for that."

"Did they?" asked Jesse.

"No, I was lucky. A nice girl befriended me. She'd been going to the school for a year so she knew the ropes and everything turned out fine. Her name was Edith Frankenthaler."

"No kidding, not Aunt Edith?" asked Jesse. "Auntie Edie is your best friend in the whole world!"

"That's right," said Mrs. Leroy. "So it just goes to show you, doesn't it?"

At dinner that night, Suzy was preoccupied, too.

"You left our bathroom an absolute wreck this morning," complained Sarabeth. "I nearly broke my leg on a dissolving sliver of soap. Disgusting! Do it once more and I'll lock you out *forever.*"

Suzy ignored her as always.

"How was your first day at Coleridge?" asked her mother.

"Did you make any new friends?" asked her father.

"I met a girl named Jesse Leroy," Suzy told them.

"What a nice coincidence," said Mrs. Pierce. "The Leroy family lives in this building."

"That means you girls will be seeing lots of each other," said Mr. Pierce.

"I don't think so," said Suzy. "Jesse didn't like me. She was awfully mean."

"I'm sure you're mistaken," said Mrs. Pierce.

"No I'm not, Mom. Jesse stepped on my new sneakers and dirtied them up."

"Why would she do that?" asked Mr. Pierce.

"She said it was to make me look like all the other

kids. She says kids at Coleridge never wear new clothes the first day. She says only geekoids do that."

Mrs. Pierce stifled a smile. "Then maybe Jesse tried to rescue you from a fate worse than death. It sounds like being a geekoid is a pretty terrible thing. Isn't that right?"

"I guess so," said Suzy grudgingly.

"Then you should be grateful to her," said Mrs. Pierce.

"And you should thank her," added Mr. Pierce.

"I'll think about it," said Suzy.

By lunch period the next day, Suzy had decided to apologize to Jesse. "You probably weren't trying to trick me yesterday. Let's try to be friends, okay?"

"Okay," said Jesse.

"Are you sure?" asked Suzy.

Jesse shrugged. "Sure, why not? I told my mom about you and she says you probably acted weird because you're scared."

"I didn't act weird," Suzy protested. "But I guess I am scared. The city scares me. It's not like Connecticut. It's nothing but big buildings. I miss the trees and flowers and animals."

"The city isn't just big buildings," Jesse told her.

"That's all *I've* seen."

"Meet me after school and I'll show you you're wrong."

"Where are we going?" asked Suzy.

"Follow me," said Jesse, as they walked several blocks up Broadway.

At 110th Street, the girls turned east and kept walking until they arrived at the Cathedral of St. John the Divine.

6

"This is the biggest church I've ever seen," said Suzy.

"It's a cathedral," Jesse corrected. "The biggest in the world. And it's still being built. See that stoneyard over there? Stonemasons are still building the two front towers." Jesse led Suzy through the grounds of the Cathedral complex. As they passed the stoneyard, several workers waved to her. "See, that's where they cut and carve the stone," she explained. "It's neat to watch them. Sometimes, they let me bang their hammers."

"You mean chisels," Suzy corrected.

"That's right. It's great to bang away at stone. You get out all your junk."

Beyond the stoneyard was an enclosed shed filled with piles of empty cans and bottles. "What's all that garbage?" asked Suzy.

"That's the recycling center," said Jesse. "My dad is a volunteer there." As they continued their walk, they reached a large stone building. "That's the Cathedral School," she explained.

"It's nice, but it still doesn't look much like the country," said Suzy.

"Just wait," said Jesse.

Beyond the school was a playground which led toward the garden. There, rosebushes trailed along a picket fence. Neatly plowed rows of vegetables grew in tidy patches. Green beans climbed trellises. Cabbage, cucumbers, tomatoes, and lettuce peeked up through the ground. "They grow this stuff for the soup kitchen," Jesse explained. "My mom is a volunteer there. And there's a flower garden over that way. And a Biblical garden, too."

Suzy saw a peacock and a rooster stroll past. A rabbit scurried from one bush into another and she heard birds singing in the surrounding trees. "This really *is* like the country."

"Sure," said Jesse. "There's lots more neat places like this in the city, too. You'll like it here." As they sat down on a bench, Jesse took a peanut butter sandwich from her knapsack. "Mom makes me carry lots of these for the homeless. Sometimes, I get so hungry, I eat some myself."

"I hate passing so many homeless people on the streets," Suzy said. "They scare me."

"Everything scares you," Jesse said lightly. "How come you moved to the city?"

"My dad made us move. He's a stockbroker on Wall Street. He said living in the city is more like being in the *real* world. Greenwich seemed real enough to me. I had my own bathroom there. Now I have to share with Sarabeth and she's disgustingly vile." Suzy began eating one of Jesse's sandwiches. "Know what? Sarabeth shaves her arms clear up to the elbows."

"No kidding," said Jesse. "Why?"

"She won't tell me."

"Calvin never tells me anything, either," said Jesse. "When I need to know something, I snoop. But who cares anyway? Calvin is a major nothing—zero brain waves, you know?"

"Just like Sarabeth," Suzy said, nodding. "No brains at all. I think she rolls her curlers too tight or something."

"Calvin curls *his* hair, too," said Jesse, giggling. "He says showering brings out the natural wave but that's a lie." Jesse suddenly realized they'd eaten *all* the sandwiches. "Now I feel guilty. But I couldn't help it, I was hungry."

"Want some carrots?" asked Suzy, digging into her

knapsack. "At home, I always carried carrots and I can't break the habit."

"Why, are you a vegetarian?" asked Jesse.

"No, the carrots were for Sebastian. He *loved* carrots." Suzy sighed. "I miss Sebastian terribly."

"Who's he, your boyfriend?"

"I can't talk about him," said Suzy sadly. "It's too upsetting."

"Okay," said Jesse, "but if we're going to be friends, we've got to tell each other personal stuff. Want me to confess something first? You wouldn't blab it around, would you?"

"No, never. I'd love to hear a secret."

"Okay. I've got a crush on Mr. MacPherson."

Suzy giggled. "Our English teacher?"

"That's right, what's so funny?"

"He's so old, he must be *thirty.*"

"So what? How old is Sebastian?"

Suzy laughed. "I don't know, but I've got a picture of him at home. Would you like to see it?"

"Sure," said Jesse. "Let's go."

Chapter Two

Jesse was really curious about Sebastian. And she was also eager to see Suzy's apartment. Ever since the building had gone co-op, rich people had moved in. Lots of them had ripped out walls, replaced floors, installed new kitchens and bathrooms.

Although Jesse loved her comfy old apartment, she was curious to see what the Pierce family had done to theirs. They had a fancy freezer with an automatic ice-maker, a microwave, track lighting, built-in shelves, a marble bathtub, and a gas fireplace. "This place is fantastic," said Jesse.

Mrs. Pierce was pleased Suzy had brought home a friend. "I'll get you girls some cookies," she offered.

"Does your mom work?" asked Jesse.

"Sure. She designs toys. What does your mom do?"

"She's a nurse. My dad owns a grocery store. Mom says he gives away most of the food to the homeless but she's just kidding."

"I never saw any homeless in Greenwich," said Suzy. "How come you've got so many here?"

"Maybe because there's none there," Jesse reasoned. "C'mon, let's see your room."

Jesse could tell lots about a person by seeing her

room. Suzy's room was neat and feminine, not at all like Jesse's, which was always a wreck.

Hanging above Suzy's bed was a photograph of a man on a horse. "That's Sebastian," she said proudly. "Isn't he the most wonderful thing you've ever seen?"

Jesse stared at the picture. The man was almost fifty, fat and bald. "No, you can't have a crush on that guy! I'll bet he's older than your father."

Suzy giggled. "No, not the guy, the *horse.*"

"Sebastian is a *horse*?" asked Jesse.

"That's right, isn't he gorgeous? Look at his gait, his stance, the way he takes the bit. Check out his muzzle and fetlocks. He's utterly perfect."

Jesse took a closer look. "He looks like an ordinary horse to me. Is he yours?"

"I wish he were," said Suzy, throwing herself onto the bed. "He belongs to the man in the picture, Mr. Bronson. He's the owner of Meadowbrook Stables." She stared up at the ceiling dramatically. "I used to ride Sebastian twice a week. I'd bring him carrots and we'd spend the afternoon together. There's no better horse in the whole world and I miss him terribly."

"I never met anyone with a crush on a horse," said Jesse.

"It was love at first sight," said Suzy.

"Have you two won prizes together and lots of horsey stuff like that?" asked Jesse.

"No, that's the tragedy of it, Jess. I've never been in a horse show—even though I once rode bareback without falling off! But I was only beginning to really learn equitation when we moved away. Mom says I'm just at that age when girls get attached to horses. She says I'll get over it but I won't, not ever."

"I know," said Jesse. "Our dog Ruffian died last

11

year and I still miss him. Sebastian isn't dead or anything but I guess you can love a horse as much as a dog."

"Much more," said Suzy. "A horse is like a person."

"So is a dog," said Jesse.

They were arguing that point when Mrs. Pierce entered with a trayful of oatbran-raisin cookies. An hour later the cookies were gone, but the girls were still talking. By five o'clock they were busy discussing their names.

"You've got a great name," said Jesse. "Suzanne Angelica Pierce sounds very fancy."

"But it won't look good on monograms," said Suzy. "When I walk into my bathroom, I'll see SAP embroidered all over."

"Who cares about junk like that?"

"I do," said Suzy.

"That's dumb," said Jesse.

"That's because your name is perfect. Jessica Winifred Leroy. JWL sounds like jewel. I wouldn't mind jewel embroidered on my towels. It's light years better than sap."

"Don't worry, you'll have a different name when you're married," said Jesse.

"No I won't. I'm keeping my own name."

"You can't do that unless you're somebody important."

"I *will* be somebody important."

"Have you got *everything* planned?" asked Jesse.

"I think so," said Suzy. "First, I'll travel. I plan to visit the Spanish Riding School in Vienna. That's where the famous Lippizan stallions come from. Then I'll become a champion horsewoman. And own my own stables. But I hope all my plans don't get ruined because I live in the city!"

"Don't bad-mouth the city," said Jesse. "It's a great place. It's got everything."

"It hasn't got Sebastian," said Suzy sadly.

Jesse couldn't argue that.

A week later, Jesse and Suzy were seated in the garden of the Cathedral after school.

"You've been in the city a while now," said Jesse. "I bet nothing scares you anymore."

"Almost nothing," said Suzy. "Only the subways, the noise, the homeless, the traffic, the dirt, and the tall buildings."

Jesse laughed. "You're hopeless."

"Nothing scares me *here*," said Suzy. "It's my favorite place in the city."

As the girls talked, several people waved to Jesse. They all hurried past the stoneyard toward the metal door opposite the recycling center.

"Where do all those people always go?" asked Suzy.

"Most of them go down into the crypt," said Jesse.

Suzy gulped. "The *crypt*? Isn't that another word for *graveyard*?"

"I don't know," said Jesse. "I've never been down there. All I know is lots of stuff goes on there."

"Like what?"

"I think there's a dance company and a theater troupe that meet there. There's an art studio, too. Mom says it's like a three-ring circus down there."

A young man waved as he strolled by. "That's Julian," said Jesse. "He's a member of the dance company." She gestured him over. "Meet my new friend, Suzy. I'm telling her about all the stuff that goes on inside the crypt."

"Did you tell her about the three dead bishops?" asked Julian.

Suzy gulped. "The what?"

"Quit it, Julian. Suzy's scared of things like that. She's from Greenwich."

"Maybe you'd like a tour of the crypt someday, Suzy?" he asked. "It's very interesting down there."

"You've never given *me* a tour," said Jesse. "Anyway, I'd rather go up there." Jesse pointed toward the tall stone turrets jutting out from below the Cathedral's gothic towers.

"Can you really climb around up there?" asked Suzy.

"Sure you can," said Julian. "The Cathedral has several levels inside. There are offices in the triforium on the second level. Beyond that there's a staircase which leads out onto the front of the building. But that's very dangerous, so you'd never be allowed to do it."

"Too bad," said Jesse, "I'd love to live dangerously."

As Julian waved good-bye, Suzy kept staring beyond the stone angels and gargoyles toward the top of St. John the Divine. "I'll bet climbing up there would feel like being in a storybook."

"Don't mention books," Jesse groaned. "We've got to start that dumbo English report soon."

"I think I'll pretend I'm Alec in *The Black Stallion*," said Suzy. "Or maybe I'll be Velvet riding her piebald horse to victory in the Grand National."

"Who will I be?" asked Jesse, sulking. "I don't read books, Suzy, I watch movies. I know I'll write a stupid report and Mr. MacPherson will hate it. And he'll hate me, too. I'd love to impress him just once."

"I'll help you," Suzy offered. "I'm good in English."

14

"No fair. Mr. MacPherson made us swear not to take help from classmates. Of course, he didn't mention family and Calvin is pretty good in English."

"You said he was an idiot."

"True, but he can do a decent fifth grade book report. And if he helps, it won't be cheating."

"Would he do it?" asked Suzy.

"Probably not."

"Maybe Calvin's not as rotten as you think."

"Are you nuts? He's barely human."

"Just like Sarabeth," said Suzy nodding. "Is it normal for us *both* to hate our siblings?"

"Sure," said Jesse. "It's part of growing up. If you don't hate your sibling you turn out warped and kill people you don't even know."

"Good," said Suzy, "I'm glad we're normal."

That night during dinner Jesse wondered if Calvin might help her with her English report. "Calvin, I've been thinking . . ."

"That's a novelty." Calvin pushed aside the plate of bread. "No bread, Mom, I can't eat carbs, they give me flabby pecs."

"I forgot," said his mother.

Jesse cleared her throat. "Calvin, I was wondering if you'd have time to help me."

"With what? Spit it out, birdbrain."

"Forget it," said Jesse. "It's *hopeless* asking you for anything!"

Calvin shot up from the table. "Got to make a call," he shouted, tripping over his feet as he dashed into the hall.

Jesse watched from the kitchen. She heard him mumbling secretively into the receiver. How suspicious. Who was he talking to?

15

Jesse grew curious. She tiptoed into the bedroom and carefully picked up the extension.

During dinner at the Pierce apartment, Suzy was telling her parents what a great time she'd had at the Cathedral.

Sarabeth kept interrupting. "I know Suzanne took it, Mother. It's my very best bristle brush and it's gone. It's impossible to share a bathroom with an incurable thief!"

"I didn't take anything," Suzy argued. Actually, she didn't remember if she had or not.

While Mrs. Pierce was settling the dispute, the phone rang.

Sarabeth blushed. "I'll get it," she insisted as she rushed from the dining room. She ran into the bedroom and slammed the door behind her.

Jesse kept giggling as she whispered into the phone. "You'll never guess what. My brother and your sister have a thing for each other."

"Sarabeth and Calvin?" asked Suzy.

"Right, isn't that a riot? What should we do about it?"

"What can we do?"

"I don't know but there's got to be a way to turn this into *fun.*"

Chapter Three

The next day the girls could hardly wait to talk together during lunch.

"What did they say to each other?" asked Suzy eagerly.

"Dumb garbage," Jesse told her. "Sarabeth sighed and giggled a lot. Calvin made his voice sound real deep. He asked your sister if she's going with anyone. She said she isn't. So they made a date to meet at Angelo's after school."

"Who's Angelo?"

"It's a pizza place. Do you want to snoop on them?"

"Isn't that awfully sneaky?" asked Suzy.

"You bet. We'll meet after school."

During their walk downtown Suzy began getting nervous again. Lots of streets they passed had major construction going on. Noisy bulldozers were parked beside cement mixers next to dumpsters overloaded with debris. Suzy was afraid to walk through the narrow pathways built underneath the scaffolding. "Something might fall on my head," she insisted. Jesse dragged her along. As she hurried through,

Suzy stopped to stare at a poster pasted along the boards.

"Don't stop, we'll be late," Jesse coaxed.

"Look, the National Horse Show is coming," Suzy said excitedly. "It's going to be at the Meadowlands and my parents promised to take me. I've been to one in Harrisburg, and to Washington D.C., too. I also went to Madison Square Garden once."

"I've never seen a horse show. What's it like?" asked Jesse.

"There are lots of exhibitions and performances," explained Suzy. "I love dressage the best."

"What's that?"

"Dressage is when the horses do fancy dance steps. There are also cross-country jumping and tandem riding. People buy horses at the show, too. Millionaires come from all over to bid on the prizewinners. It's real exciting, Jess. If you'd like to go, I bet my parents would get you a ticket."

"I guess so. But now let's hurry to Angelo's."

"Why does everyone in the city have to *hurry* all the time?" asked Suzy.

When they arrived at Angelo's, Jesse and Suzy picked a corner booth where they wouldn't be noticed. They could safely spy on Calvin and Sarabeth from a distance.

"What're they doing now?" Suzy whispered.

Jesse peeked over the back of the booth. "They're biting into the same slice of pizza."

"Disgusting."

"Now there's cheese dribbling down their chins."

"What're they saying?" asked Suzy.

"Calvin's bragging about his pecs."

Suzy nodded. "Sarabeth likes guys with muscles."

18

"In their *heads.*" Jesse watched intently. "Now they're exchanging goo-goo eyes. What's your sister see in him? I'd love to tell her how loathsome Calvin looks in the morning. And his feet smell!"

"Sarabeth belches at breakfast," Suzy confided. "She'd *die* if she knew I told that."

Jesse slid back into her seat. "I'll bet we know lots of gross things about them both," she observed. "If we were smart we'd use this junk to our advantage."

"How?" asked Suzy with interest.

"Blackmail," Jesse whispered. "Let's threaten to reveal their worst secrets if they refuse to do our bidding. That way, I'd get Calvin to help write my report."

"I'd get Sarabeth to lend me her makeup," said Suzy. "She has gobs of it but she hides it somewhere." Suzy fidgeted with the napkin cannister. "But it won't work, Jess. They'd have to be crazy about each other before they'd worry that we'd reveal their stupid secrets."

"Let's keep spying on them," Jesse suggested. "Then we'll know if they get crazy for each other."

"Maybe we should form a club," said Suzy. "That would make things more official and less sneaky."

"A club for snooping?" asked Jesse. "That sounds promising."

That evening in Jesse's room, the girls worked out the details.

"I think a club sounds too much like kid stuff," said Jesse.

"Then let's form a society," Suzy suggested.

"That sounds better. What'll we call it?"

"How about The Secret Snoop Society?"

"That sounds great," said Jesse. "Our first plan of action will be to spy on Calvin and Sarabeth."

"But that's not all we'll do," said Suzy. "Our society should also perform good deeds and things like that."

"What for?"

"Because it's important," Suzy insisted. "I refuse to consider myself a plain old noseybody."

"Okay," Jesse agreed.

"Let's write a charter," said Suzy. "All proper societies have a charter."

Jesse agreed to that, too. "As long as *you* write it," she said. Scrambling through her messy desk, she found some clean paper.

Suzy began writing. . . .

We the undersigned do herewith form The Secret Snoop Society. We do hereby agree to check out, investigate, track down, trace, and otherwise inquire into any activity which we think important to our lives, liberty, and pursuit of happiness. Being of sound mind, we swear to stick by each other through thick and thin. Under pain of expulsion, we swear never to reveal the purpose of our society to another living soul. We do hereby agree to all this and sign our legal names.

Jessica Winifred Leroy
Suzanne Angelica Pierce

When it was signed, Jesse read it out loud.

"Let's get it xeroxed so we'll each have a copy to hang on our wall," said Suzy.

"No, we've got to keep it hidden," Jesse cautioned.

"You're right," Suzy agreed. "We'll each keep a copy under our bed."

Chapter Four

Once The Secret Snoop Society was formed, the girls' lives suddenly changed.

Suzy spent less time missing Sebastian. Jesse didn't think as much about Mr. MacPherson.

They were both too busy spying on their brother and sister.

The boring, everyday things Sarabeth and Calvin did had suddenly become of great interest. Every time Calvin got a phone call, Jesse listened in. Every time Sarabeth bought new makeup (which seemed to be every minute), Suzy wondered whom she wanted to impress.

Suzy and Jesse kept notes about their arrivals, departures, and any change in habits. They even wrote down what their siblings wore each day. To avoid suspicion, the girls agreed to be *nice* during their snooping period.

Jesse stopped making nasty remarks about Calvin's meager muscles. Suzy stopped borrowing all of Sarabeth's things.

After a few days, Sarabeth and Calvin grew suspicious.

"Why are you being so sweet to me?" asked Sarabeth.

Suzy didn't know what to say. "I guess—maybe I *like* you."

"Oh," said Sarabeth, quite stunned.

Calvin wanted to know the score, too. "What's up, creepball? You haven't bad-mouthed me in days."

Jesse smiled at him innocently. "I guess I'm growing up."

Calvin sneered. "It's about time."

After a week of extreme niceness, the girls grew discouraged. Was it worth the effort? Sarabeth and Calvin hadn't done anything romantic.

"What a bust," Jesse grumbled. "All they do is hang around the water fountain. No dates, nothing."

"Hardly passionate," said Suzy.

"Deadly boring," said Jesse. "Let's drop this whole idea."

But on Friday, everything changed. The girls were snooping around behind the school lockers as usual—spying on Calvin and Sarabeth as they stood by the water fountain—when Jesse finally heard something interesting.

"Make sure nothing goes wrong," Sarabeth insisted. "Tell no one. I'll call you tonight." Then she hurried away.

"What's up?" asked Suzy eagerly. "What did they say?"

"I think it's real important," said Jesse. "And real secret. We'll find out more tonight."

Later that night when Sarabeth called Calvin, Suzy was listening on the extension. The conversation was short but she heard every word.

"It's all arranged for Saturday morning," said Sar-

22

abeth. "Let's meet by the clock in Grand Central Station."

"Why don't we go downtown together?" asked Calvin.

Sarabeth sounded nervous. "No, I have other stops to make. Anyway, we shouldn't be seen together. Certain people—well, you know. Besides, it's an awfully big responsibility."

"You can't pull it off *alone,*" said Calvin.

"Of course not. But it's my job to find out all the details. To make sure there aren't any problems."

"No loopholes, right," said Calvin. "That's important."

"Then it's all set? Ten o'clock by the clock."

"Don't worry, I'll be there."

Afterward, the girls phoned each other instantly.

"Why are they meeting downtown?" asked Suzy. "Where do you think they're going?"

"Who knows?" said Jesse. "Let's find out!"

Saturday morning, Suzy was awfully nervous. In the three weeks she'd lived in the city she still hadn't been on the subway.

"Relax, it's no big deal," said Jesse.

Mrs. Pierce was pleased Suzy was finally attempting it. "Your father thinks it's a wonderful idea." She handed Suzy a twenty dollar bill. "In case you see something you want to buy downtown."

In the elevator, Jesse jabbed Suzy. "Why'd you tell your mom about Grand Central Station? You gave the whole deal away."

"I only told her we were taking a subway," Suzy explained. "Why do you suppose Calvin and Sarabeth

23

are meeting in Grand Central Station? Do you think they're eloping?"

"That's stupid. They've only had one lousy date."

"Sarabeth is very flighty," said Suzy. "She fell in love with her swimming teacher after one lesson. She's afraid she'll be an old maid. Sarabeth says after eighteen, it's downhill for females. She already uses wrinkle cream. Did you know they make special cream just for eye wrinkles?"

"Calvin uses muscle cream," said Jesse.

"See, they're made for each other," said Suzy.

As the girls walked down Broadway toward the subway, Suzy got nervous again. "There's another one of *them*," she said, pointing to a ragged homeless man standing by the subway entrance.

Jesse took a peanut butter sandwich from her pocket and handed it to him. The man stared at it as they hurried down the subway steps.

A loud clatter from the incoming train sent chills through Suzy. "Can't we take a cab instead?"

Jesse dropped her token into the turnstile. "Stop complaining. My folks taught me how to travel alone so I'm real good at it. You'll learn, too."

Suzy didn't think so. Everyone on the subway seemed threatening. When they got off at 42nd Street they hurried onto a shuttle train where crowds of people pushed and everyone stepped on Suzy's feet. Suzy almost lost Jesse in the crunch and nearly panicked. It was hard to imagine that someday this would seem *easy*.

When they reached Grand Central Station, Calvin was already standing underneath the giant clock, combing his hair.

Jesse watched with amusement. "That dope took two showers this morning."

24

Sarabeth entered the station. She ran toward Calvin and kissed his cheek.

"Sarabeth locked herself in the bathroom all morning," said Suzy. "She curled, moussed, and tinted. I'll bet they're eloping."

"They've got no luggage," said Jesse. "Something else is up."

Calvin and Sarabeth approached the ticket counter. They bought two tickets, then hurried toward Track 19.

Jesse glanced at the schedule board above the counter. "The train on that track goes to Connecticut."

"One of the stops is Greenwich," Suzy noted. "I'll bet that's where they're going."

"We've got to catch that train," said Jesse. "It's lucky your mom gave you money."

The girls bought two round-trip tickets for Greenwich. They boarded the train just as it was about to pull out. They walked through the cars until they found Calvin and Sarabeth. Then they took seats in the car behind them.

"Maybe Sarabeth is taking your brother on a nostalgic visit to the scenes of her childhood," Suzy suggested.

"That's sappy," said Jesse. "Calvin hates the country. He says it's filled with bugs and bozos. Besides, we don't know for sure they're getting off at Greenwich."

"I bet they do," said Suzy.

She was right. As the train pulled into Greenwich, Calvin and Sarabeth headed toward the door. The girls quickly followed. As they stood on the platform, Suzy sniffed the country air. "I'm homesick already," she said, sighing.

Then Suzy saw something which made her doubly homesick. A pick-up van from Meadowbrook Stables was parked outside the station. She recognized the driver. It was Roscoe, one of Mr. Bronson's grooms. Suzy's heart leapt. She longed to go to Meadowbrook and ride Sebastian.

The girls watched as Sarabeth waved to Roscoe. Then she and Calvin climbed in back of the van and they drove away.

"They're going out to Meadowbrook," Suzy said. "We've got to follow them."

"We'll have to walk," said Jesse. "We've got no more money. How far is Meadowbrook?"

"Who knows? It may be miles," Suzy whined. "People in Greenwich don't walk." She sat on a bench outside the station and started sulking.

"Yoohoo," someone shouted from down the street. "Is that you, Suzanne?" the voice called out.

Suzy looked up. It was Mrs. Hotchkiss, a former neighbor, driving by in her station wagon. "What on earth are you doing back here? Did you miss us so much you had to come back?"

"We need to get to Meadowbrook," Suzy explained. "It's important; can you take us there?"

Mrs. Hotchkiss pulled up alongside them. "Meadowbrook?" she asked, laughing. "You didn't miss us at all, did you? You miss that horse you grew fond of." She smiled knowingly. "I remember what that's like."

"Can you drive us out there?" asked Suzy.

"Of course, it's only a mile from here."

"Suzy didn't know how far it was," said Jesse. "She says people here never walk."

"She's right," said Mrs. Hotchkiss, opening the car door. "Thank goodness they don't have to."

Chapter Five

"This place stinks," said Jesse.

"That's not a stink, it's an aroma," said Suzy. "The best aroma in the world."

"It smells like poop to me," said Jesse.

"It's horse manure," Suzy corrected. She loved the sound of the words. "Nothing smells as good as horse manure."

"Want to bet? Where do you think Calvin and Sarabeth disappeared?"

"If they're here, I'll find them." Suzy led the way past the jumping fences and beyond the closed riding corrals of Meadowbrook. Halfway toward the stable area, she noticed Calvin and Sarabeth in the distance, talking to Mr. Bronson. She and Jesse quickly ducked behind a tree to watch.

"Can you hear them?" asked Jesse.

"They're too far away."

"Maybe your sister came to ride a horse. Maybe she misses Sebastian, too."

"Sarabeth doesn't ride," said Suzy. "Besides, she's wearing high heels. What fool wears high heels to a stable? Something's fishy."

The girls watched as Sarabeth kept talking. Soon Mr. Bronson started nodding.

"I think they're making a deal," Jesse observed.

"What business could she have with Mr. Bronson?" Suzy wondered.

The girls cautiously crept closer so they could hear the end of the conversation.

Mr. Bronson looked serious. "No, I can't get involved in that business. You'd better handle it yourself." Then he walked away toward the paddock.

Sarabeth looked real upset. Calvin put his arm around her. "Relax, no sweat," he said. Then they walked past the field toward the stables.

"I wonder what happened," Jesse whispered.

"This is weird," said Suzy. "They're visiting the horses. Sarabeth hates horses."

The girls continued to keep out of sight as they followed along behind. Suzy stopped to watch a stableman take several horses out of their stalls. She glanced at them eagerly, hoping to see Sebastian, but he wasn't there. Another stablehand threw bales of hay down from the hayloft, then broke them up to fill the hay bins. Three of the school horses waited patiently at their stall doors. They began soft nickering noises to attract the attention of the stablehand measuring out their grain. Sebastian wasn't among them.

"Someone must've taken Sebastian out for a ride," said Suzy wistfully.

"That poopy smell is getting stronger," complained Jesse.

"This is where the school strings live," Suzy explained. "They're Mr. Bronson's horses. Boarders are kept in a separate stable where their owners can care for them. Mr. Bronson boards lots of prizewinners during the horse show circuit."

As they approached the boarding stables, Sarabeth and Calvin came back into view. This time, Sarabeth was talking to a tall, thin man in large, dark sunglasses. He wore an expensive suit and shiny, pointed shoes.

"I've never seen him here before," said Suzy.

"He looks suspicious," said Jesse.

Suzy agreed.

The girls ducked behind the fence to listen. During the conversation, they heard Sarabeth mention money several times. Lots of money. Sometimes, Calvin interrupted to say "cool" or "great" or "how's about it?"

The man in the shiny shoes spoke very softly so they couldn't hear him.

"He looks super sneaky," whispered Jesse. "I bet he's a crook."

"Sarabeth doesn't know any crooks," said Suzy.

"I'll bet Calvin knows lots of them," said Jesse.

"I hope your brother isn't leading my sister into a life of crime," said Suzy.

"Let's wait and see," said Jesse.

When they'd finished their conversation, Sarabeth gave the sneaky man a piece of paper. Then Shiny Shoes shook hands with Calvin. After that he hurried away. The girls watched him get into a bright red Porsche parked behind the stable. A cloud of dust blew up behind him as he speeded down the road.

"Remember," said Sarabeth, "not one word about this or you'll ruin the entire plan."

"No sweat," said Calvin.

Then he and Sarabeth left Meadowbrook. And they left Suzy and Jesse behind—more confused than ever.

* * *

As they walked back to the station, Suzy kept complaining. "I can't believe I was at Meadowbrook and never saw Sebastian. What cruel irony."

"Knock it off, Suz, we've got more important problems. What's this mysterious plan all about?"

Later that afternoon the girls sat in Jesse's room arguing.

"I think we should disband," said Suzy dramatically.

"We can't," Jesse protested, "we've got a charter."

"We'll tear it up. Being noseybodies brings trouble. And I didn't even get to see Sebastian!"

"You can quit," said Jesse, "but I'm not giving up until I find out what's up."

For a long time Suzy sat in sulky silence. "Do you think they're really involved in a crime?" she finally asked. "Sarabeth has always been so well-adjusted. She never has problems. *I* do all the complaining."

"She can't be too normal if she likes Calvin," said Jesse.

"Then it's our duty to save her from herself," Suzy reasoned. "There are too many crooks in this city already."

"And I'd like to get some dirt on Calvin," Jesse added. "So let's examine our facts. I'll write down everything we know."

"Okay, then we can form conclusions," said Suzy.

The girls wrote down every detail they'd observed that morning. They noted the snatches of conversation with Mr. Bronson and Shiny Shoes. When they finished, they read it aloud.

Jesse was disappointed. "It all adds up to *zero.*"

"We'll have to keep snooping," said Suzy. "Let's write out our plan of action."

"Okay. First, let's keep listening in on all phone calls. Whatever the setup is, C and S plan it over the phone."

"That's right," Suzy agreed. "So let's not arouse their suspicions about us. Let's pretend we don't care anything about them."

"That'll be easy," said Jesse.

Suzy wrote down their continued plan of action.

THE SECRET SNOOP SOCIETY PLAN

We must both continue to follow Calvin and Sarabeth wherever they go together. We must both listen in on the extension whenever Calvin and Sarabeth talk on the phone together. We must both continue to be *nice* to Calvin and Sarabeth, no matter how hard or disgusting it gets.

Agreed to by: Jesse Leroy
Suzy Pierce

"That's great," said Jesse, signing it. "Now let's eat, I'm starving."

"So am I," said Suzy. She threw the paper on her bed and they both ran into the kitchen to raid the refrigerator.

Late that night, Calvin got a phone call from Sarabeth.

"It's all arranged," Sarabeth whispered.

"Are you sure it's safe?" asked Calvin.

"It's far too dangerous to be safe."

"Sure, you're right. If word gets out about this deal, we won't stand a Chinaman's chance of pulling it off."

"Don't mention Chinamen, not ever again," Sara-

31

beth cautioned. "Remember to keep your mouth zipped about *everything*."

"Okay. Right. So when do we meet?"

"Tomorrow. Two o'clock in Central Park. By the statue of Alice. Be on guard. Expect the unexpected."

"That's cool," said Calvin. Then he hung up.

"I'm scared," Suzy whispered nervously into the phone. "What's going on?"

"Isn't it great?" said Jesse. "Things are finally heating up. We'll have some super clues soon. See you tomorrow, don't be late."

Chapter Six

"Do you see any Chinamen?" Jesse peered out from behind the trees surrounding the statue of Alice In Wonderland. Toddlers crawled around the base as older children clung to the Mad Hatter's hat or climbed to the top of Alice's head.

"It's not proper to refer to people that way," Suzy corrected. "Say Chinese or Asian."

"Okay, do you see any?"

Suzy glanced toward the miniature boat pond where several children were racing their sailboats. There was an Indian man wearing a turban walking by, but she didn't see anyone who looked Chinese. "No. Why are you looking for one?"

"I'm not sure," Jesse admitted. "It's something Calvin said on the phone. Keep your eyes open, okay? I've a hunch nothing is what it seems to be in this deal."

Three boys on bikes whizzed by, nearly knocking Suzy over.

"I'm trying to watch but it's so crowded here," she said.

"Crowds are good, we won't be seen," said Jesse.

She checked her watch. "It's almost two-fifteen, where are they?"

Suzy spied someone familiar. She saw a girl seated on the bench beside the statue. The girl was wearing large sunglasses and a trenchcoat. Her face was almost hidden behind an open newspaper. Suzy recognized her red suede boots. "That's Sarabeth in *disguise*. Why is she hiding?"

Jesse glanced around. She saw someone familiar, too. A young man lay on the grass beside the statue with an open magazine covering his face. Jesse recognized the raggy Pumping Iron decal on his faded denim jacket. She looked closer. "That's Calvin!"

Suddenly Sarabeth peeked over her newspaper. Then Calvin peeked out from under his magazine. Their eyes met. They stood up but they didn't approach each other. Instead, they walked to opposite sides of the boat pond.

"Why are they pretending they don't know each other?" asked Suzy.

"This is getting weird," said Jesse.

A short old man wearing a baggy gray suit and carrying a violin case slowly approached the statue. He opened his case. He removed a violin and one banana. He ate the banana. Then he propped up the empty case and began to play the violin. He smiled to himself as sweet, romantic waltz music filled the air. People strolling by smiled back. Lots of them dropped bills and coins into his case.

Calvin walked by and dropped something into the case, too. But it wasn't money. It was a folded-up slip of yellow paper. Then he hurried toward the entrance of the boat house.

"Did you see that?" asked Suzy.

Suddenly, Sarabeth approached the old man. She

glanced furtively from side to side. Then she dropped another piece of folded-up paper into his case. After that, she hurried in the direction of the museum.

"Do you think it's a message?" asked Suzy.

"Maybe the old guy is their *accomplice,*" said Jesse.

"Which one should we follow?" asked Suzy.

"Forget them both, let's get the evidence."

Pushing their way through the crowds, the girls ran toward the old man. They stared down into his case. Two notes lay among the dollar bills, dimes, and quarters. Jesse bent down to grab them. As she did, a woman shouted from behind her, "Stop, you little thief!" The woman lunged toward Jesse and Suzy screamed hysterically. The old man quickly stopped playing. When he saw what was happening, he grabbed his violin case and slammed it shut.

Before the girls could escape, a policeman rode by on his motor scooter. "What's wrong?" he asked.

The woman pointed an accusing finger at Jesse. "See this girl? She tried to steal this poor old man's money."

"That other girl is her accomplice," someone else added.

"No I'm not," Suzy protested.

"He's the accomplice," Jesse argued, pointing at the old man.

"Me?" he asked. "I'm a *musician.*"

"Shame on you," said the woman. "Why pick on a poor old man bringing beauty into the park?"

The policeman looked confused. "Did these girls take anything?"

The old man looked confused, too. "I don't want trouble. I only want to play Strauss."

The policeman stared at the girls sternly. "Okay

35

you two, move along. Don't let me catch you here again."

Jesse and Suzy started to run. They didn't stop running until they'd reached the exit of the park.

When they arrived home, Suzy's face was still red with embarrassment.

"Let's go to my house to plan our next move," Jesse suggested.

"I'm going home," Suzy grumbled. "I need a bubble bath real fast. It's an emergency!"

Suzy pounded on the bathroom door. "Let me in."

After what seemed like forever, Sarabeth opened it. She stood in the doorway wearing her terry cloth robe, a towel wrapped around her head, looking calm and collected. "I've been in the tub for absolutely ages."

Suzy knew that was a filthy *lie.* She'd seen Sarabeth skulking out of Central Park. "That's not true and you know it!"

Sarabeth threw her a haughty glance. "What do you know about it? And what's it your business, if you please?" With a smug grin, she walked down the hall and slammed her bedroom door behind her.

"Now she's a *liar* and a crook," Suzy moaned. "We never should have left Connecticut!"

Chapter Seven

The next day in the lunch room the girls never took their eyes off Calvin and Sarabeth.

Calvin kept showing off his muscle control by balancing milk cartons on his biceps. Sarabeth kept giggling and gasping as the cartons bobbed up and down.

"Face it," said Jesse, finishing her tuna sandwich, "my brother is a major dweeb."

"And a bad influence," Suzy added. "Whatever's going on, it's all his fault. Sarabeth never did anything illegal until she met him. She's not smart enough to get involved in anything criminal."

"Neither is Calvin."

Suzy pushed her lunch aside. "It's this city, it corrupts people. Normal humans turn into beasts."

When Jesse finished her lunch, she began eating Suzy's. "I thought about this all night. Remember that old man in the park? He's a little fish just like Calvin and Sarabeth. Which means Shiny Shoes is the big fish. Everyone else is just a thingamajig—like in chess."

"A *pawn*? You think our siblings are pawns in some larger criminal plan?"

37

"Sure. I bet Calvin would do anything for money. He's desperate to buy gym equipment."

"Sarabeth is dying to buy a dress that costs a fortune. She also wants a beauty make-over. Mom says it's silly but Sarabeth insists it's vital for her mental health." Things were starting to add up to Suzy. "They've both sold their souls for cash. Only so far, we haven't seen them do anything illegal. Dropping notes in a violin case isn't against any law."

"The plot's still thickening," said Jesse, "which means the Snoop Society has to watch them even closer."

"Open yourselves," said Mr. MacPherson, "and let the world of literature enter. I hope each of you has selected the book you plan to use for your report."

Jesse hadn't. She stared dreamily into Mr. MacPherson's eyes. They were definitely the bluest she'd ever seen. Bluer than the sky, for sure. And his brown, curly hair looked so soft she wondered if *he* used rollers, too. How old was he? Maybe he was still in his twenties? Maybe he wouldn't be absolutely ancient when she was grown up? Maybe he wasn't married?

"Maybe you could pay attention, Jesse Leroy?"

"Sorry, Mr. MacPherson," said Jesse, blushing.

"I'm glad we have the afternoon off," said Suzy. "Snooping has become major work."

Jesse agreed. "With Calvin at basketball practice and Sarabeth at the dentist, we finally have time to ourselves."

Suzy sighed. "I never imagined the Snoop Society would become a full-time job."

The girls decided to stroll through the Cathedral

Close. It had become their favorite after-school hangout. Suzy and Jesse stopped to admire the Peace Fountain at the entrance of the grounds. Four sprays of water cascaded down a pedestal at the base of the sculpture. Above the water were a smiling sun, a sleeping moon, several animals, a giant crab, and an angel carrying a man's head.

"I like it but I don't understand it," said Jesse.

"I don't understand it either," Suzy admitted.

A man walking by noticed their interest. "It's an allegory," he explained. "It represents peace. That giant crab refers to our origins in the sea. The sleeping moon is tranquility. It's set against the joyous smiling sun rising in the east. Next to the sun, a lion and a lamb relax together in the peace of God's kingdom, just as foretold by the prophet Isaiah."

"What about the giraffes?" asked Suzy.

"Giraffes are the most peaceable of animals," the man explained.

"Why did the angel lop someone's head off?" asked Jesse. "That doesn't seem peaceful."

"That's the warrior archangel Michael vanquishing evil," he said.

"How come you know all that?" asked Jesse.

"I'm the sculptor. My name is Greg Wyatt."

"Really? How did you ever build something so big?" asked Suzy.

"It was sculpted in my studio inside the crypt. It's a very *large* studio."

"I told you neat things happen down there," said Jesse.

"Yes," Greg agreed, "the crypt is home to several artistic projects. That's the true function of a cathedral. In medieval times it was the place for festivals and a circus of activities, so it's nice to know some things don't change, isn't it? A cathedral should always be a sanctuary from the world, shouldn't it? After all, remember Quasimodo."

"Who's he?" asked Jesse.

"The hunchback of Notre Dame, that's who," said Greg. "He was the main character in a famous novel. You should read it someday." Greg glanced approvingly at his own creation. "Yes, a sanctuary, that's what this place is."

"I like your statue a lot," said Suzy. "Thanks for explaining what it means."

"You're welcome," said Greg. "Come visit my studio sometime if you like," he offered, then waved good-bye.

"Wouldn't you like to snoop around the crypt?" asked Suzy.

"Not today," said Jesse. "I promised Mom we'd pick veggies for the soup kitchen."

As the girls entered the vegetable garden two volunteers handed them baskets. Within minutes all thoughts of the outside world drifted from Suzy's mind. As she picked green beans she occasionally snapped a few to test their freshness. Greg was right, she thought, the Cathedral was a sanctuary.

When they'd finished, the girls sat on a bench in the flower garden. Jesse ripped open a huge bag of potato chips and Suzy took out a magazine.

Jesse groaned. "Not another horsey mag. Don't you ever read about people?"

"There's a great article in here about AliFarabi. He's a thoroughbred Arab stallion who traces back to the original Godolphin Arabian."

"Fascinating," said Jesse, more interested in potato chips.

"AliFarabi is showing at the National Horse Show

this year. If he wins, his owner plans to sell him. A win at the show will add a million dollars to his price."

Jesse glanced at the photo. The sleek, brown stallion had a neatly braided mane and tail. His rider was dressed in a flowing desert cape with colorful tassels. "Why's that guy wearing a funny outfit?"

"This picture was taken when AliFarabi was performing in the Native Costume Event. Isn't he beautiful?"

"I thought you were in love with Sebastian," said Jesse.

"I can't resist a handsome horse," said Suzy. "Sebastian is wonderful but Ali is spectacular. I can't wait to see him perform. My parents got you a ticket to go with us."

Jesse couldn't get too excited. "Thanks," she said, gobbling down her chips.

That night during dinner Sarabeth dribbled food all over her chin. "It's the Novocain," she said sullenly. "I can't chew properly. My life is in a total shambles."

"Two cavities isn't terrible," said Mr. Pierce.

"It's disastrous," argued Sarabeth. "I'm *degenerating*. My teeth are rotting and my skin is sagging. What's worse, the dental receptionist called me 'Ma'am.' I've got to take that beauty make-over, Mother. It's a vital emergency."

Suzy sat in nervous silence. She knew her sister's make-over would be financed with illegal money!

At 11 P.M., Sarabeth called Calvin.

Jesse had already gone to bed. Luckily, she wasn't

asleep yet. By the third ring, she was listening on the hall phone.

"It's going according to plan," said Sarabeth. "It's all arranged. I'll get it tomorrow."

"Where is it?" asked Calvin.

"In the Metropolitan Museum. Be there by three o'clock. We meet at five."

"Where?"

"I'll contact you," said Sarabeth.

"Okay, that's cool," said Calvin.

Chapter Eight

Jesse hated museums.

"It's cold as death in here," she complained.

"Is that guard watching us?" asked Suzy nervously.

"If he had sense, he'd watch your sister. Sarabeth's the one who's come to steal."

"Don't *say* that," Suzy whined.

The girls had passed a large crowd in the Great Hall but the Egyptian Wing was almost empty. The rooms seemed cold and grim as they walked past alabaster urns, a large sarcophagus, and stacks of burial linens brown with age.

A security guard paced up and down, eyeing each visitor. Sarabeth stood alone in the center of the gallery, staring into a case containing a gold leaf necklace.

Jesse and Suzy hid behind a corner display filled with rows of canopic jars. Each jar was made of pottery and shaped like a mummiform figure with a female head stopper.

"Hey, these are sort of nice," said Jesse. "Are they for cookies?"

"No way," said Suzy reading the sign. "They contained viscera removed during the embalming process."

"What's viscera?"

"Liver and guts, I guess."

Jesse cringed. She glanced into an adjoining case. Lots of painted eyes stared back at her from a wooden coffin belonging to someone called Hapyankhtifi. "Your sister better make her move soon. Hanging around this mummy stuff is giving me the creeps."

"You really think Sarabeth plans to *steal* something?" asked Suzy. "This is horrid. It's a major deal to steal from this place. Sarabeth will be an old woman before she gets out of jail. Who wants an old jailbird for a sister? What if she gets shot by that guard? Everything here is hooked up to alarm systems so she'll never escape alive." Suzy suddenly felt faint. She leaned against the glass display case. "I think I'm hyperventilating!"

As the security guard passed he looked at her sternly. "No touching the cases."

"Snap out of it," said Jesse, watching Sarabeth leave the gallery. "Hurry, we can't lose her now."

The girls followed Sarabeth through the Egyptian Wing, past the Temple of Dendur, back into the Great Hall. There they battled the converging crowds hurrying up the main stairs.

"We've been tailing her for an hour," Jesse grumbled. "I hope she knows where she's going."

Sarabeth entered the Arts of Ancient China Gallery. She passed the Bronze Age artifacts, ignoring them. When she reached the rooms with art from the Han Period, she stopped to stare into a case.

"This is weird," said Suzy. "She's staring at an empty space."

Although the case was empty, Sarabeth stared into

it for a long time. Then she retraced her steps back through the galleries. Before following her, Suzy took a fast glance into the display case. The sign inside read: Temporarily Removed—Woman on Horseback—Ming Dynasty.

The girls followed Sarabeth as she hurried down the steps to the Great Hall. They watched her drop a note into a potted plant then hurry away. Suzy kept lookout while Jesse quickly read the note then replaced it in the plant. Then they ran to catch up with Sarabeth as she entered the Greek sculpture hall.

"What did the note say?" asked Suzy.

"Meet me at A.W."

"What's that mean?" asked Suzy.

Sarabeth entered the American Wing.

"That's what it means," said Jesse, growing anxious. "Is your sister taking an all-day tour of this joint or what? There's no sign of Cal or Shiny Shoes. You think we've got this whole deal figured wrong? If something sneaky doesn't happen soon, I'm leaving."

Sarabeth entered the Period Rooms. She paused outside a Gothic Revival library room taken from a 19th century house in Connecticut. Standing behind the wooden partition, she admired the furniture. An old lady was admiring it, too.

"Beautiful, isn't it?" asked the old lady.

"Beautiful," Sarabeth agreed.

"She's lying," Suzy whispered. "Sarabeth despises anything that doesn't come from Conran's. What's she up to?"

When the old lady left, Sarabeth took another note from her purse. She slipped it underneath the lamp on the mahogany side table, then left.

That's when the girls noticed Calvin stroll down the corridor. He approached the library. He removed

45

the note from under the lamp. He read it, then stuffed it into his jeans. As he walked toward the elevator, the note slipped from his back pocket. Jesse dashed down the corridor and snatched it up.

It said: The Main Gift Shop—5:15—That's where we make the switch.

"Their meeting place," said Jesse.

"What switch?" asked Suzy.

"Let's find out!"

On weekends, the Gift Shop of the museum was always very crowded—especially before closing time. Customers eager to make last minute purchases stood crammed on lines beside all the cash registers.

Jesse couldn't believe the crunch. "Are they giving stuff away?"

"I hope we don't get trampled." She spied Calvin and Sarabeth. "Look, they're up there by the counter."

Sarabeth asked to see a clay figure inside the display case. The salesgirl removed it. As Sarabeth admired it, the girls pushed closer.

"I'll take it," said Sarabeth.

The salesgirl replaced the statue in the case and got another one from under the counter.

"No, I want *that* one," said Sarabeth. "I want the one you just showed me."

"That's our display copy," said the salesgirl.

"I don't care, I want it."

"But they're all alike," explained the salesgirl.

"So give me the one I want," said Sarabeth.

"There's no difference," the salesgirl insisted.

"What's holding things up?" asked people on back of the line.

Calvin leaned against the counter. "Listen up, okay? She wants *that* one. Get it?"

The salesgirl grew nervous. She unwrapped the statue in the box and put it in the display case. Then she removed the other statue from the case and placed it in the box. She rang up the sale, then slipped it into a shopping bag.

"It's done," said Sarabeth, grabbing the bag.

"Good, let's split," said Calvin.

Within a moment, Calvin and Sarabeth had disappeared into the crowd of people pushing toward the front doors of the museum.

Suzy was really confused. "They didn't steal anything, after all, did they?"

Jesse wasn't sure. "They must've done *something* illegal."

Halfway home, Jesse was still trying to figure things out. "Something's definitely fishy."

"You're right," Suzy agreed. "Why should Sarabeth sneak around the museum? Why'd she make a fuss about that statue?"

"I'll bet the statue isn't what we think it is," Jesse reasoned.

"What *is* it?"

"This reminds me of *The Maltese Falcon.*"

"What's that?" asked Suzy.

"An old movie. Sometimes movies help me figure out stuff in real life. Yeah, it may be an important clue."

"To what?"

"I don't know, Suz, I'll have to watch the movie again. Let's pick up a copy at the video store."

* * *

When Jesse walked into the Video Vault, everyone in the place waved hello.

"I'm their best customer," she explained. "Ken, the manager, says my head lights up when a new video is released."

Jesse walked down the aisle marked Classics and found a copy of *The Maltese Falcon.* Then she saw a copy of *The Hunchback of Notre Dame.* "Look, it's about Quasimodo, that guy Greg mentioned. Let's watch it, too, okay?"

"Greg said to read the book."

"You know I don't read books."

"Don't remind me," said Suzy. "That's what started this whole snooping business. Isn't it ironic? We formed the Snoop Society to get dirt on Calvin so he'd help you write a book report."

"Yeah, ironic," said Jesse, taking the videos to the cashier.

Chapter Nine

The girls stuffed themselves with popcorn as they watched *The Maltese Falcon.*

Suzy loved the story of the infamous black bird and how people lied, cheated, stole, and killed to get their hands on the priceless statue. "What a great old movie."

"See what I mean?" asked Jesse. "The Maltese Falcon wasn't what people thought it was. The guys who thought it was fake found out it was real. And the guys who thought it was real discovered it was fake. A clever crook had made a super switch."

"Yeah, so?"

"So maybe we've discovered a switch, too. In which case our siblings are in deep trouble."

"Don't say that, Jess."

"Face facts, Suz. I'll bet Shiny Shoes works at the museum. He removed the original statue from the case and replaced it with that sign. But he knew he couldn't escape with the stolen loot. So he put the statue in the gift shop where there's a replica on sale. Then he hired Calvin and Sarabeth to buy the statue. Only they didn't buy a replica, they bought the *original.* And they walked out without anyone knowing."

"No," Suzy insisted, "Sarabeth can't end up like the woman in that movie. Maybe she's stupid, but she'd never commit a crime."

"You can't ignore the facts," said Jesse.

"You haven't got all the facts," said Suzy. "Maybe the statue Sarabeth bought isn't like the one missing from the case. We never saw that one."

"That's true," said Jesse. "Where could we find out what it looks like?"

"Dad says you can find anything at the library. Maybe there's a picture of it in an art book."

"And if we find a picture of the statue, and it *is* like the one in the museum shop, we have our evidence."

"Okay," Suzy agreed, "we'll visit the library after school tomorrow."

It was after midnight and Jesse couldn't sleep. Knowing that Calvin was involved in a major theft filled her with mixed emotions. Would she really be happy to see him in jail? No, all she wanted was to *scare* him just a little. And how about Mom and Dad? It'd break their hearts to learn that Calvin was a criminal.

Jesse grew bored lying awake so she got up and went into the living room. She switched on the TV and slipped *The Hunchback of Notre Dame* cassette into the VCR. She loved the movie. Poor, dumb, disfigured Quasimodo, the pathetic bell-ringer of Notre Dame Cathedral. He wanted to be understood, but he wasn't too smart. Then he fell in love with a pretty girl and ended up a criminal. In the end, only the great Cathedral offered him sanctuary.

Jesse was touched. Calvin was a lot like Quasimodo, she thought. So maybe St. John the Divine could be *his* sanctuary. If the cops came to grab him, maybe she could hide him down in the crypt, or in the stoneyard. Sure, she could bring him food and clothing. She'd be his eyes to the outside world. She'd . . .

"That stupid TV woke me up," said Calvin, stumbling into the living room. He yawned and scratched his behind. "Turn it off right now, scuzzbrain, or I'll deck you."

Jesse angrily switched off the set. Let Calvin go to prison! Let him rot there *forever!*

"We've got to do it today," Jesse argued. She and Suzy were seated in the lunch room. "Every minute counts. Who knows when they'll turn over the stolen merchandise. Once the deal is finalized and they get *paid,* old C and S are officially criminals!"

"But the statue is still in the hall closet," Suzy assured her. "Sarabeth will be at the dentist, so she can't do anything criminal. Mom is making me go, too, Jess; I can't help it."

"Okay," said Jesse, sulking, "we'll do it tomorrow."

"No, you're right. We can't waste time. *You* do it."

"Me? Go to the library by myself? You've got to be kidding!"

"It's no joke. We need information fast. Go after school and find out about that statue."

As Jesse walked into the Bloomingdale Branch of the New York Public Library, she felt uneasy. She disliked the aroma in the air. It smelled like old wood, old books, and old paper from old trees.

"May I help you?" asked the librarian.

"I need an art book."

51

"Anything in particular?"

"Something with lots of Chinese stuff in it."

"All our art books are in the 700 section," explained the librarian.

As Jesse walked down the 700 aisle, she glanced at all the art books. She couldn't find anything about the Ming Dynasty or the little clay statue.

"I can't find what I want," she told the librarian. "You should set up this place like a video store. I always find what I want there."

"We have a different system," said the librarian, smiling. "What are you looking for?"

"I need a picture of a statue. It's a woman on a horse from the Ming Dynasty."

"Maybe you'll find that at Donnell, the main art library."

"Where's that?"

"Fifty-third Street, off Fifth Avenue."

Jesse groaned. "I have to visit two libraries in one day? I don't believe it!"

The Donnell Library was much bigger, newer, and livelier. And the art research section had lots more books. There were long tables to read at and Xerox machines for making copies of the artwork. Jesse found a book with lots of information about Chinese art. As she took notes she noticed a sign on the wall. A movie was being screened in the auditorium at six o'clock, as part of a Charles Laughton Festival. It was *The Hunchback of Notre Dame*. Jesse thought it was a neat idea to show movies at the library. She was anxious to see the movie again, this time on a big screen. But she'd have to finish her research first. Hurriedly, she thumbed through the book, hoping to find the information.

It was after eight o'clock when Jesse returned home.

"I couldn't believe it when you called," said her mother. "Research at the library? *You*?"

Jesse shrugged. "It's no big deal."

"Suzy's been calling for hours. You'd better call her back."

"You'd better eat dinner first," said her father. "It's fish—brain food for our new scholar."

"Quit teasing. One trip to the library doesn't make me a freak or a genius."

"What took you so long?" asked Suzy, hurrying Jesse into the bedroom.

"There was lots to learn, okay? I was lucky the library was open late. I had to wade through gobs of dynasties."

Jesse proudly read through her notes. "There was Shang and Chou and Ch'in. Ch'in is when the Great Wall of China was built. Then there was Han and T'ang and Sung and Yuan. Sounds like a Chinese rock group, doesn't it?"

"What about the *statue*?" asked Suzy impatiently.

Jesse handed her a Xerox picture of the clay horse and rider. The caption read: Woman on a horse, Metropolitan Museum of Art.

"It's the same statue," Suzy gasped. "That must mean Sarabeth has the original. But I still can't believe it. There was nothing about a theft on the news."

"The museum doesn't know about it yet," said Jesse. "Like it or not, our siblings are two rotten apples."

53

"No," Suzy shouted, hurrying from the room. "I can still save her from a life of crime."

"What can *you* do?" asked Jesse, hurrying after her.

"I'll *return* the statue," Suzy explained. She opened the hall closet and stared at the empty space on the shelf.

The statue was *gone.*

At 11 P.M., the phone in the Leroy house rang.

By now, Jesse and Suzy knew a late call probably involved Calvin and Sarabeth. As usual, Jesse grabbed the extension.

"It's time to finish our business," said Sarabeth.

"Great," said Calvin. "Where?"

"In Chinatown. On Mott Street."

"When do we meet?"

"Five o'clock tomorrow. Broadway and 110th Street. Outside the subway station."

"That's cool," said Calvin.

"Why can't you go?" asked Suzy as she and Jesse left school the next day.

"I've got to be at the soup kitchen," said Jesse. "I always fill in when Mom's on a case. If I don't go I'll have to explain why. It'll give the whole show away."

"Is that the *real* reason?" asked Suzy. "I'll bet there's another free movie at the library."

"What if there is?" said Jesse. "It's *Mutiny on the Bounty* but I'm not going."

"Are you sure? I bet you *want* Calvin to be in big trouble."

"Maybe I do," Jesse admitted, "but he's no good to

me in jail. Honest, Suz, I can't go. You'll have to do it alone."

"Me? Go to Chinatown alone? You must be joking!"

"This isn't funny. You've *got* to do it!"

Chapter Ten

The sunglasses Suzy borrowed kept sliding down her nose. The fedora hat was too big, too. And her mother's jacket was much too long. All in all, Suzy looked like the world's shortest spy. Borrowing her mother's clothes hadn't been such a great idea. But it was better than no disguise at all. What if Sarabeth spotted her? What if Calvin chased her down a dark, deserted Chinese street? Better safe than sorry, no matter how stupid she looked.

As she waited outside the subway station, an uncontrollable itch crept across her body. When would Calvin and Sarabeth arrive? Suzy bought a magazine at the newsstand, then buried her face inside it.

After a while, she began getting nervous. The ragged homeless man was in his usual spot by the subway entrance. He kept watching her. What did he want? Why did all the homeless always stare? As Suzy tried to avoid his glance, she nearly missed Calvin and Sarabeth's meeting. They were already halfway down the steps when Suzy noticed them. She adjusted her fedora and hurried after them.

On the subway Suzy hid her face behind her magazine. Snooping from over it was hard. Did real spies actually do it? Suzy decided to watch Calvin and Sarabeth's *feet* instead of their faces. Calvin's red joggers and Sarabeth's blue leather boots were unmistakable.

The train stalled near the 28th Street station and sat there for several minutes. Suzy got worried. She didn't dare peek over her magazine. Across the subway car, the red joggers and blue leather boots began fidgeting. Then the red joggers stood up. They walked across the car toward Suzy. They stopped in front of her. Would she be unmasked, detected, accused? No, Calvin was checking the subway map above her head. Thank goodness her identity was still secret!

When they reached Canal Street, Sarabeth and Calvin got off the subway and Suzy followed. Things looked awfully dark outside. Suzy removed her sunglasses. It still looked dark. Night was beginning to fall. Suzy grew scared. She was downtown, in the dark, in a strange neighborhood. Was Sarabeth worth this much trouble?

Calvin and Sarabeth walked east several blocks, then turned downtown. The neighborhood took on an Oriental flavor. Suzy noticed signs above the food stores written in calligraphy. People with foreign faces and clothing pushed by her. Exotic aromas spilled out of the storefronts. In the poultry markets, rows of plucked dead ducks hung upside down in windows. In the novelty shops, gaily painted wooden dolls in Chinese robes sat on shelves, their heads bobbing up and down, as if laughing at the passersby.

This was nothing like Connecticut. Suzy yearned for the security of a brightly lit shopping mall!

She found it hard keeping up with Calvin and Sarabeth. The streets were so narrow and crowded, Suzy nearly lost them several times. When they arrived at Mott Street, it began to rain. Suzy watched as store owners brought in their vegetable bins. She glanced at the odd collection of roots and sprouty things. Suzy didn't like Chinese food, even though Sarabeth kept telling her it was fabulous. Suzy liked foods she recognized. She didn't like eating things she couldn't pronounce. "You'll grow up to be a culinary idiot," Sarabeth was always telling her. Suzy didn't care. She still loved burgers and fries.

The Chinese storekeeper held up one of the misshapen roots. "You want buy?" he asked, smiling through his broken teeth.

Suzy shook her head nervously and hurried down the street. She saw Calvin and Sarabeth entering Ming-Sum-Loo Restaurant on the corner.

As the rain kept falling, Suzy wished she could follow them inside where it was warm and dry. Instead, she watched them from the window. The restaurant was almost empty. Two Chinese men sat hunched over bowls of steaming soup. Calvin and Sarabeth didn't sit at a table. They stood and waited. Several minutes passed, then an old Chinese man wearing a green brocade robe appeared. He bowed and gestured them into the back room.

Suzy pressed her face against the window. Was the Chinese man their contact? What was in the back room? Was this the meeting place with Shiny Shoes? Where was the box with the statue in it? Did Sarabeth have it with her? To her horror, Suzy realized *she hadn't noticed.*

As it continued to pour, the fedora hat dripped rain into Suzy's eyes. Her clothes were soaking wet. She'd get pneumonia, for sure. What was worse, she'd bungled the investigation, lost track of the vital evidence. What would Jesse say? And what about Sarabeth? She was in that back room, probably handing over the stolen statue. Her sister was already a *criminal.* This trip had been for nothing; she'd *botched* it.

Twenty minutes passed while Suzy stared through the window. Calvin and Sarabeth never came out. Ten more minutes passed. They still didn't come out. Then a horrid thought struck Suzy. There must be *another exit.* Which meant Calvin and Sarabeth were gone. Which meant Suzy was *alone.* Alone in Chinatown with no cab fare!

As Suzy hurried down the street, she tried not to panic. She ran several blocks, then looked around. Was she heading toward the subway or away from it? The streets weren't numbered, so it was hard to tell. Had she gotten twisted around? She turned and ran in the other direction.

By now, the rainy streets were almost deserted. Suzy saw an old Chinese woman near the corner and ran toward her. "Do you know where the subway is?" The woman bowed and nodded, but she couldn't speak English.

Suzy saw a man approaching. He wore a shabby coat and ragged trousers. At first, he looked familiar. She quickly realized it was the universal costume of the homeless that she recognized. Finally, Suzy's fear of being lost won out over her fear of homeless people. She spoke to him. "I can't find the subway. Can you tell me where it is?"

The man nodded but didn't stop. Suzy followed him down the block. "Is it this way?" she asked.

The man pointed down the street. "Over there," he said. "Don't talk to no more strangers. And be careful."

Suzy almost cried with relief when she saw the subway steps. After paying her fare, she hurried onto an uptown train. She sat shivering in her wet jacket, eager to return to her warm, dry apartment. Then she realized she hadn't thanked the homeless man. For a moment, Suzy wondered where he'd spend the night.

Chapter Eleven

The next day, Jesse and Suzy were seated in the school cafeteria.

"Don't shout at me," Suzy pleaded, "it's almost my birthday."

"What's that got to do with it?" asked Jesse sternly.

"People should be nice to each other near birthdays." Suzy sneezed into a tissue. "Besides, none of this was my fault. And I nearly *died*, too."

"How could you botch up a simple trip to Chinatown?"

"I guess you had to be there, which you should've been." Suzy sneezed again. "I hope I won't be sick for the horse show."

"Don't change the subject," Jesse scolded. "You botched a simple snoop and missed the illegal switch in Ming-Sum-Loo."

"Maybe Mr. Ming owns the statue," Suzy offered. "Maybe it was stolen from him and now he's got it back."

"Get real. Mr. Ming must work for Shiny Shoes, too. They're laundering that statue just like crooks launder money. They're trying to cover their tracks.

I see stuff like that in movies all the time." Jesse poked at her chocolate pudding and watched it wobble. "You've messed up the case, so now I can't blackmail Calvin. I've no evidence."

"Don't blame me for everything," Suzy pouted. "After all, I'm having . . ."

"A birthday, yeah, you told me." Jesse sighed. "Oh well, I guess I'll get my usual F in English—thanks to *you*."

"It's not my fault you're rotten in English," Suzy snapped. "Maybe if you'd read a book sometime instead of always watching movies . . ."

"Look who's giving me advice," said Jesse. "A person who can't do anything right. I can't believe you botched a simple snoop assignment."

"It wasn't simple. It was cold and wet and dark and . . ."

"Quit finding excuses, okay? Face it, we have no evidence of anything. Which means the Snoop Society is *dead*."

"That's fine with me," Suzy replied. "We wouldn't have needed a society in the first place if you didn't have a crooked criminal brother!"

"Hold it," said Jesse, "don't blame all this on Cal. Your stupid sister is the one who started it all."

Suzy stood up and stared at Jesse haughtily. "I think I'd like to go now."

Jesse glared back at her. "Don't let me stop you."

Suzy left the cafeteria. Jesse kept poking at her pudding until she smacked it so hard it turned into mush.

At dinner that night, Suzy had no appetite.

"You haven't eaten a thing," said her mother.

"What's wrong, are you sick?" asked her father.

"I had a fight with Jesse Leroy," Suzy explained, "and I never want to see her idiotic face again!"

"Oh dear," said Mrs. Pierce, "how awkward. We're all going to church together on Sunday. It's the Feast of St. Francis and there's a special service at St. John the Divine. Mrs. Leroy says it's a wonderful service in which animals surround the altar. I told her we'd all be going."

"*I* won't go," said Suzy.

"Yes you will," said Mr. Pierce sternly. "It sounds like a lovely event and I want you to see it."

"Okay, I'll go," said Suzy, sulking, "but if Jesse Leroy is there, I won't have a good time, I promise."

"This place looks like a zoo," said Calvin, "and it sounds like one, too."

As the Leroys walked down the aisle of the Cathedral, meows, chirps, barks, and strange exotic noises filled the air. The lively chorus of animal music echoed clear to the altar. Hundreds of people filled the church and many had brought their pets to be blessed. There were cats in carriers, hamsters, gerbils, mice, and birds in cages. Dogs of all sizes were on leashes. There were turtles in boxes, goldfish bowls, and parrots perched on people's shoulders. Ferrets crawled in and out of their owners' jackets and some people had snakes wrapped around their necks.

"Isn't this wonderful?" asked Mrs. Leroy.

"I think the animals look forward to this service," said Mr. Leroy. "They're all so well behaved."

Jesse poked Calvin. "They've got more manners than you, musclehead."

Calvin poked her back. "Dry up, creepball," he replied.

"People bring their pets from all over the city," Mrs. Leroy explained.

"Calvin punched me," Jesse grumbled.

"Drop dead," Calvin mumbled.

"Behave yourselves," said Mr. Leroy. "Can't you take a lesson from the animals?"

Jesse watched as a woman pushed a shopping cart loaded down with three cat carriers. Each carrier had prizewinning ribbons pasted to the front.

"They must be show cats," said Mrs. Leroy.

"That's some smart lady," said Calvin knowingly. "A special blessing will give her cats the winning edge in their next competition."

"Don't be silly," said Mrs. Leroy. "Priests will bless *all* the animals later on Pulpit Green."

Jesse felt a twinge of sadness. "I wish we still had Ruffian. Will they bless a dead dog, too, Mom?"

"We'll find out, dear."

As the Pierce family entered the Cathedral, Jesse cringed. "You didn't tell me *they* were coming. Are they sitting next to us?"

"Of course," said Mrs. Leroy. "I saved them seats."

"I heard you and Suzy are mad at each other," said Mr. Leroy. "But I bet this service makes you change your mind. If all these animals can get along without fighting, two girls should be able to manage it."

Jesse wanted to argue that point but she couldn't. She would have to explain what she and Suzy had fought about, and that would mean telling Dad about the Secret Snoop Society, which she couldn't do, either. It would also mean telling Dad that Calvin was a slimy crook and thanks to Suzy she had no evidence of that.

The Pierce family took their seats beside the Leroys. Calvin and Sarabeth threw each other furtive glances. Jesse and Suzy ignored each other.

The service began. First, dancers dressed in white ran down the aisles carrying colorful banners representing the four elements of Creation: air, water, earth, and fire. Then the strange musical sounds of humpback whales, harp seals, spotted owls, elephants, and wolves filled the Cathedral through the loud speakers. After several hymns, Bishop Moore delivered the sermon. He told about the life of St. Francis and his love for all living things. "When you return home," he concluded, "observe the light of God shining through your pet's eyes."

Suzy nearly cried. She had no pet of her own so she thought of Sebastian.

There were more hymns and prayers. After Communion, Bishop Moore announced the most sacred part of the service. "The silent procession is about to begin."

The Great Bronze Doors were opened. Suddenly, a magical stillness filled the Cathedral.

Suzy turned to look as the majestic animal procession began to enter. She didn't know what to expect. At first, a huge gray-brown mass which looked like a heaving mountain appeared in the doorway. As it slowly lurched forward, she realized it was an *elephant*. Not just a baby elephant but a full-sized one, plodding down the center aisle.

Accompanied by a handler, each animal slowly climbed the stairs of the West Front. It entered the Cathedral and proceeded down the aisle toward the central altar. The congregation all watched in respectful silence.

A camel entered, followed by a horse and then a llama. Gradually, the animals grew smaller. A young woman held a chimp clinging to her shoulder. A man carried in a baby pig. A lizard resting on a pillow was carried in and so was a rat. Someone else wheeled in a beehive. A man had a falcon resting on his arm. A small boy carried a bowlful of algae and a girl carried a tiny fir tree. All forms of life were represented.

"This is wonderful," Suzy whispered.

"I knew you'd be glad you came," said Mrs. Pierce.

"See how all the animals get along?" whispered Mr. Pierce. "Not like some people."

Suzy got the point. In this magical moment, she couldn't stay mad at Jesse. She tapped her on the shoulder. "Isn't this great, Jess?" she whispered.

"It's not bad," said Jesse, smiling. "I'll see you in the garden later, okay?"

Suzy sighed with relief. They were *friends* again!

After the service, several clergy gathered on Pulpit Green to bless the animals. Dean Morton didn't object to blessing Ruffian, even though Jesse told him the dog had been dead for a year.

"I want Sebastian blessed, too," said Suzy. "He's not *my* horse but I love him."

Dean Morton obliged. Then Suzy and Jesse walked around the grounds. They admired all the animals in the special petting zoo which had been assembled for the day.

"Now that we're friends again, I think we should start snooping again, too," said Suzy.

"No, the Snoop Society is dead," said Jesse. "Nothing personal, but you botched the whole case."

"Maybe I didn't," said Suzy. "Maybe you figured things wrong. Maybe *you* botched everything."

"How do you figure? And do you want to be friends again or what?"

"I'm merely suggesting we don't know all the facts yet," said Suzy. "We never found out why Calvin and Sarabeth went to Meadowbrook, did we? That's what started this whole mystery, isn't it?"

"Sure, I guess so, but . . ."

"But we don't know *why* they went there, do we? So maybe there's still lots we don't know. So maybe we can still turn our siblings away from their lives of crime."

"Forget it," said Jesse, "that wasn't my plan. I wanted to *nail* Calvin, not help him."

"Well I want to help Sarabeth," said Suzy. "I don't want a crooked sister. What about when I'm famous someday? What if the newspapers find out about her?"

Jesse groaned. "Still planning your future?"

"C'mon," Suzy coaxed, "let's keep following them a while longer. We might learn something."

"Maybe," said Jesse, reconsidering. "And maybe we'll catch them spending their illegal money. Then maybe I'd have concrete evidence against crummy Cal."

"Then maybe you could convince him to get therapy," Suzy suggested.

"Are you kidding? Cal would drive a shrink crazy! Anyway, why should I save his skin?"

"Maybe he'll be grateful and do you a favor?"

"Okay," Jesse agreed, "so maybe the Snoop Society *isn't* dead yet."

Chapter Twelve

"Maybe we shouldn't have bothered," Jesse grumbled. "We brought the Snoop Society back to life but now there's nothing to snoop."

For three days, things had been absolutely dead. Calvin and Sarabeth never called each other. They didn't have any more sneaky conversations by the water fountain, either. In fact, they rarely spoke to each other at all.

Every day after school, Calvin resumed his ritual of pumping iron. And Sarabeth locked herself in her room—"catching up on work," she said.

"Everything's too normal," said Jesse.

"And too quiet," Suzy agreed. "Sarabeth doesn't fight with me anymore, not even when I leave soap dissolving in the tub."

"Maybe she's being nice because it's near your birthday?"

"Everyone *forgot* my birthday," said Suzy, sulking. "They're all too busy this year. No one has mentioned it and it's almost Saturday."

"Don't be silly."

"They forgot," said Suzy angrily. "Mom and Dad

always ask me what I want, but no one asked me anything."

"Those tickets for the horse show are for Saturday," said Jesse. "I guess that's your present."

"That's not fair," she argued. "I would've gotten horse show tickets anyway. A present is something you wouldn't have gotten anyway." Suzy sighed wistfully. "This never would've happened in Connecticut."

That night Suzy sulked all through dinner. No one noticed. Sarabeth was far too preoccupied. Mr. Pierce was too busy. He'd brought home tons of work and was eager to begin. Mrs. Pierce was too upset. All her new appliances had short-circuited the old wiring. She'd waited all day but the electrician had never come to fix it. The dishwasher wasn't working so Suzy was elected to do the dishes.

As Suzy scrubbed out all the greasy pots and pans, she felt like Cinderella. Maybe she should use Cinderella for her school book report. Why should she write about horses, anyway? Horses were part of her wonderful old life in Connecticut. She would never see horses again now that she lived in the city. In fact, the only horse Suzy had seen had been in the Cathedral!

With every dish she scrubbed, Suzy felt more sorry for herself. She was *worse* than Cinderella. At least Cinderella had a fairy godmother. Suzy had nobody. Disgusted, she stared at the potato peelings overflowing the trash can. Was she expected to clean that up, too? No, it was Sarabeth's job to dump the garbage. "Sarabeth!" she shouted, but her sister didn't answer. Grumbling to herself, Suzy dragged the trash out to the back door. She dumped it into the large plastic bag resting by the service elevator. As she did, a patch of paper at the side of the bag caught her eye. It was a note addressed to Sarabeth and it was written in Calvin's handwriting. Was this why there hadn't been any phone calls lately? Had the siblings switched to writing?

Excitedly, Suzy grabbed the note from the trash. She wiped off the food remnants, then flattened it on the ground to read it:

Hey Sarsy,
How's it going? I think the little creeps still have a tap on the line. No sweat, we can ditch them. Get me the vital stats by tonight—time, place, you know. We'll pull off this deal without a hitch.
And don't worry, I won't blow it.

Cal

Suzy couldn't wait to call Jesse. "Meet me by the garbage bags outside your back door. Right away!"

"It's no use," said Jesse. "We've looked through three bags of garbage and there's no note."

"There has to be an answer," said Suzy. "In Calvin's note, he asks for information, so Sarabeth had to reply. Do you think he has it in his pants pocket?"

"When did they discover we were snooping?" Jesse wondered. "I guess Cal is sneakier than I thought." She stared at the garbage bags. "We're wasting our time out here. If crumbo Cal is onto us, he wouldn't throw Sarabeth's note in the trash. He'd either tear it up, eat it up, or ditch it in the toilet."

"But we've got to find out what it said. You're the

69

movie expert, Jess. How do they find out these things in mystery movies?"

Jesse thought a minute. "They'd check the pad the note was written on. Sometimes, a pencil impression is left on the next sheet of paper. Can you sneak into Sarabeth's room and steal her notepad?"

"I'll try," said Suzy.

Later that night, Suzy and Jesse met again in the back hall. Suzy had sneaked into Sarabeth's room and taken the next sheet of paper on her notepad. Jesse lay it on the ground, then blacked it out with pencil. They read the note:

Dea- Ca-,
    You'-- right- it isn't saf- to us- th- pho--. Things are go--- fine. Who woul- have guessed? I never di- thing- like thi- in Con--------. Now I --ve a taste for it. And I'm ready fo- the big dea-. It's all set for Satur---. If this doesn't wo-- ou-, we'll lose big mon--. Meet me outsi-- the Claremont Academy at 89-- an- Amster---. Ten o'clo--. That's when o-- precious shipment arri---. Isn't th-- fu-?

                                        Yours,
                                        Sar----h

"I guess they're like vampires," said Suzy solemnly. "Now that they've tasted crime, they can't stop."

"Yeah, this must be a whole new crime," said Jesse.

"What'll we do about it?"

"Follow them, naturally."

Chapter Thirteen

It was a crisp autumn morning. "The beginning of apple cider weather," Mr. Pierce had said. The kind of day that always made him happy.

But Suzy wasn't happy. Her stomach churned and her legs felt like rubber bands. She felt a sense of impending doom as she and Jesse walked to 89th Street.

"Jess, I peeked in on Sarabeth last night. She was wearing her sleep mask and snoring. Know what? She looked *evil.* Do you think it's genetic? Will I become a crook, too, when I become fifteen?"

"Cal acted real innocent this morning," said Jesse. "When Mom asked where he was going, he said he was helping a friend plan a surprise. I nearly choked! He's learned to tell real whoppers."

Suzy started feeling panicky. "Let's not follow them, okay? Who cares what they're stealing? What we don't know won't hurt us."

"This is an official Society snoop," said Jesse. "There's no turning back."

"But what if Sarabeth is too far gone for therapy? I'll be responsible if she spends her life in jail. That's too big a burden."

"You'll deal with it. What do you figure they're stealing from a place called Claremont Academy? It must be a school, so maybe it's got expensive computers."

"Or rare old books," Suzy suggested.

Jesse was getting eager to learn about Calvin's latest crime. She checked her watch. It was 9:45. "We've got to get there early to find a place to hide."

When they arrived at 89th Street, Jesse saw an old-fashioned sign announcing CLAREMONT RIDING ACADEMY in large gold letters.

"Is this a driving school?" asked Jesse.

Suzy's heart pounded as an unmistakably familiar smell filled the air. "They must teach horseback riding here. Which means they have a *stable*. I didn't know there was a stable in Manhattan."

"Neither did I," said Jesse. "What could Cal and Sarabeth steal from this place?"

As Suzy ran down the block, the delicious smell of horses continued to greet her. She couldn't believe it. This was a real riding stable tucked away on an ordinary side street. Beside the three-story brick building was a large open area with dirt covering the ground. It was a fully equipped riding ring! A woman wearing livery was putting her horse through paces and practicing jumps.

Suzy noticed an office adjoining the ring. "Do you really give riding lessons here?" she asked.

"Yes," said the woman inside, "we have daily classes in Hunter, Dressage, Jumping, and Side Saddle."

"Where are the stables?"

"Upstairs."

"Are they *real* stables?" asked Suzy hopefully.

"We're the oldest stable in the country," explained

72

the woman. "We have over one hundred horses. We also offer boarding facilities."

The woman dressed in livery circled the riding ring, then led her horse to the entrance. "Excuse me, we'd like to pass," she said.

Suzy stepped aside and watched the horse and rider slowly trot down the side street, past the parked cars and piles of garbage stacked up for the Sanitation Department. She felt she was dreaming. Why hadn't someone told her about this place? She'd been afraid she'd never see riding horses again and here were dozens right under her nose! "Isn't this wonderful, Jess? It's a real ring and a real stable and everything. Maybe my parents will let me take lessons here."

"Sure, it's great, Suz, but we've got business, remember? Your sister is coming soon. She's ready to steal a precious shipment of something."

"What could she steal from a riding academy?" Suzy wondered.

"Hide," Jesse cautioned, "here she comes!"

The riding ring was empty so Jesse and Suzy hid in the corner and watched. As Sarabeth approached the entrance of Claremont Riding Academy, she stood and waited until Calvin came down the street. Then they both stood waiting at the sidewalk. Soon, a horse trailer drove down the block and stopped outside the riding school.

"What's that thing?" asked Jesse.

"That's how they transport horses," Suzy explained. "Inside, there's a stall, just like in a stable." She read the side of the van. "It's from *Meadowbrook.*"

"Great, that's the missing puzzle piece. Now we'll find out why C and S went up there."

The driver parked the trailer, removed a portable

73

ramp, and placed it under the trailer door. Then a red Porsche slowly cruised down the block and parked behind the trailer.

"It's Shiny Shoes," said Suzy.

Shiny Shoes got out of his car and approached Sarabeth.

"Everything has been arranged," said Sarabeth.

"No hitches?" asked Shiny Shoes.

"No sweat," said Calvin.

The driver of the trailer opened the door. Carefully, he guided a horse down the ramp, keeping close to its shoulder.

The girls watched as a dark brown horse emerged from the trailer. It wore quilted pads tied around its legs, knee wraps, and a head protector which also acted as blinders.

Despite the horse's disguise, Suzy recognized it. "That's *AliFarabi!*" she whispered.

"Who?" asked Jesse.

"That's the valuable horse scheduled to perform at the National Horse Show tonight."

"What's he doing here?"

Suzy's heart sank. "I guess he's the precious shipment Sarabeth mentioned in her note. He must have been stabled up at Meadowbrook."

Jesse nodded. "Maybe that means Shiny Shoes hired Sarabeth and Cal to steal him."

"No, my sister isn't a horse thief," Suzy protested. She ran from the riding ring to confront Sarabeth. "Don't do it," she shouted.

Shiny Shoes backed off nervously. "Who's that kid?"

Jesse ran after Suzy. "Come back!" she insisted.

"Hey, there's another one," shouted Shiny Shoes. "What's up? What's going on?"

Sarabeth glared at Suzy. "What are *you* doing here?"

Calvin threw Jesse a filthy look. "Snooping again, creep?" He nudged Sarabeth. "I was afraid we wouldn't shake those little leeches."

"Sarabeth, don't *do* this," Suzy pleaded.

"It's all arranged," said Sarabeth angrily. "Why did you have to spoil everything?"

The woman from the office approached. "You'll have to sign some papers before your horse is officially boarded at Claremont," she explained. "Then you can take Sebastian up the ramp and see that he gets settled in his stall."

The girls watched as Sarabeth, Calvin, and the driver followed the woman back into the office.

"She called that horse *Sebastian,*" said Jesse.

Suzy called after the woman. "Wait, you've made a big mistake. That horse isn't Sebastian. It's Ali-Farabi."

The woman didn't hear her. She had already closed the office door behind her.

But Shiny Shoes heard every word. "Hey, I think maybe you kids know too much. That could be real bad for your health."

"I know you're trying to turn my sister into a crook," said Suzy. "But I won't let you. Why is she pretending that horse is Sebastian? What is Ali-Farabi doing here? He's supposed to perform at the horse show tonight."

"You've got lots of questions, don't you kid?" asked Shiny Shoes. "Take my advice and don't get answers. Just stay cool and everything'll go real smooth like we planned."

"Like *who* planned?" asked Jesse. Things had gotten too confusing. "What does Aliwhozee have to do

75

with the Chinese man in Ming-Sum-Loo or the stolen statue? Are C and S really stealing a million-dollar horse?"

"I warned you about asking questions," said Shiny Shoes. "Let's all be real polite and no one'll get hurt, okay? Just play along with this deal and everything'll be fine. Horsey gets a nice cozy stall to cool his heels and no one's the wiser, see?"

Jesse nudged Suzy. "Didn't you tell me Aliwhatshisface increases in value if he wins the horse show?"

"That's right. His price goes up one million dollars."

Jesse nodded. "Maybe I've figured things out. Cal and Sarsypoo aren't horse thieves, they're *horsenappers*. Get it? Shiny Shoes wants to change the odds. He wants Alibaba out of the running."

Shiny Shoes moved closer. "I should've known I couldn't trust dumb teenagers with nosey kid sisters. You squirts won't keep your mouths shut, will you?"

Suzy glanced frantically around the riding ring for help. It was empty. She glanced toward the office door. It was still closed. She tried to scream but Shiny Shoes quickly covered her mouth. Jesse tried to run but Shiny Shoes grabbed her, too. Then he pushed them both up against the wall. "You squirts won't say anything and you know why?" He slipped his hand into his pocket and removed a pocketknife. "You know what I can do with this?"

"Slit our throats?" Jesse gasped.

Shiny Shoes smiled menacingly. "Nah, that wouldn't be smart and I'm a real smart guy. You two blab and guess what? That fancy horsey gets his ankles slit. One slash and he don't ride anymore, get it?"

Suzy glanced toward AliFarabi. He was standing

by the entrance of the riding ring, still wearing his protective head pads and eye shields. Suzy knew the horse was completely defenseless against attack.

"Just one cut and it's all over," Shiny Shoes continued. "A little accident, that's all. Who knows, maybe you kids'll get blamed for it. You shouldn't snoop around where you don't belong. That looks real suspicious."

"No, don't hurt the horse," Suzy pleaded.

"I see you get the picture," said Shiny Shoes. "Yeah, this might work out okay. Keeping you kids scared is good insurance. You'd like to keep that horse healthy, right?"

"We won't say a word about anything, we promise," said Suzy.

Shiny Shoes loosened his grip. "Okay, that's better. I'm going in the office now to make sure all the papers get signed. But remember, one false move and my knife finds a home in that horseflesh. So stay quiet."

Jesse watched Shiny Shoes walk away. "He's got us trapped," she whispered. "He's smarter than I thought. Now we've got to go along with this deal or else."

"Not if we find a way to protect Ali," Suzy suggested. "Shiny Shoes thinks we're too scared to make a move."

"And he's right. If we open our mouths, he'll attack the horse."

"Not if we rescue him first," said Suzy.

"How can we do that?" asked Jesse.

Suzy glanced toward AliFarabi. Beyond the entrance where he stood, an old crate lay on the side street waiting to be picked up by the Sanitation Department. "I think I have an idea," she said. "Follow me."

Suzy ran to the sidewalk and picked up the crate. She carried it toward the entrance and shoved it next to the horse. Then she climbed up on the crate and mounted AliFarabi.

"Are you nuts?" Jesse shouted. "What are you doing?"

"I'm rescuing this horse. C'mon, hurry, I'll help you up."

Jesse froze. She stared up at Suzy who looked so high and far away seated on the horse. She glanced toward the office. Shiny Shoes was coming out the door.

"Hey," Shiny Shoes shouted, hurrying toward them. "What are you kids doing?"

"C'mon," Suzy insisted, extending her hand to Jesse. "Climb on the crate and I'll give you a boost."

"Doesn't this guy have a saddle or something?"

"There's no time to saddle him up. Don't be scared. I told you I once rode bareback."

"But I've *never* ridden."

"Hurry up," Suzy coaxed.

There was no time to waste. Just as Jesse climbed onto the crate, Shiny Shoes reached them. She thrust one leg over the horse, then Suzy leaned down and gave her a final boost up.

Suzy quickly removed the horse's head protector pads and threw them aside. She grabbed the reins and kicked in her heels. AliFarabi whinnied in protest, then rose up on his front legs.

"Get off there," shouted Shiny Shoes, trying to grab the reins away from Suzy. AliFarabi whinnied louder, shook his head frantically, then knocked Shiny Shoes to the ground.

Before Jesse knew what had happened, the horse was galloping down the side street!

Chapter Fourteen

"I'm dying!" Jesse shouted. "Slow down!"

"Hang on," said Suzy, "you're doing great."

"I think I lost my stomach," Jesse groaned. She felt awful. Sitting on a moving horse was a terrible thing. Her head kept shaking, her stomach kept churning, and her rear end kept aching. As she clung to Suzy's waist, she stared down at the ground. Everything looked far away and weird. "Can't you slow this guy down? I thought you knew how to ride."

"I do," said Suzy, "but I guess Ali has never ridden in city traffic. And neither have I."

"I'm scared!" moaned Jesse.

Suzy was scared, too. When they reached the traffic light, she couldn't get the horse to stop. Luckily, the signal was green and no one was crossing the street. But Suzy knew she wasn't in control. AliFarabi weaved, wobbled, and refused to take the bit. As he raced down the street, Suzy saw another stoplight coming up. This one was *red*. "Maybe I made an awful mistake," she cried. "Maybe we'll all get killed!"

Jesse felt like she was on a roller coaster. "This is awful, do something," she pleaded. She stared at the approaching red light. "It's like in all those movies where everyone drives off a cliff!"

Suzy kept pulling at Ali's bit. She frantically dug in her heels harder and sternly repeated several commands. Ali finally slowed down to a trot. Then as Suzy pulled in his reins, he came to a stop.

Suzy breathed a sigh of relief. She leaned over and patted Ali's flank. "I think I know how to handle him now, Jess. He favors his left side and he likes strong commands."

Jesse turned around and looked behind them. There was a red Porsche two blocks away. "Uh-oh, Shiny Shoes is on our tail. What'll we do?"

"We could ride into Central Park. But maybe we'd better find a safe place to hide Ali. If we don't get him off the streets soon I'm afraid he'll get hurt. And so will we."

"Where can we hide a horse?"

"There must be a safe sanctuary somewhere," said Suzy.

"Let's take him to the Cathedral Close," said Jesse. "Can you shake Shiny Shoes?"

"Are you serious? I managed to make Ali stop and go but he doesn't know how to shake criminals."

Jesse glanced around again. The red Porsche was only one block away now. "He's gaining on us, let's hurry."

"Okay, hang on tight," said Suzy. Now that she knew how Ali liked to be handled, she felt more confident. When Ali angled left, she quickly pulled him back into control. Suddenly, the ride became exhilarating. By the time they reached 98th Street, the horse had worked up a good speed. "Isn't this great fun?" asked Suzy.

Jesse felt like throwing up.

When they approached the crosswalk at 110th Street, Suzy made the horse slow down to a trot. "Is Shiny Shoes still behind us?"

"We lost him," said Jesse, as they approached the Cathedral grounds. "He'll never suspect we brought a horse in here."

Inside the quiet Cathedral Close, away from the street confusion, Ali grew more relaxed.

"He likes it here," said Suzy. "I bet he thinks it's more like country."

Jesse peered beyond the hedges and stared at the street outside. The red Porsche was nowhere. "We gave him the slip. We're safe at last."

Suzy rode Ali around the grounds until they reached the stoneyard. "I still think we should hide Ali somewhere until we can reach his owner."

"Let's take him into the crypt," Jesse suggested.

Suzy gave Ali a friendly pat and dismounted. Then she helped Jesse get down. Jesse's rear end tingled and her legs felt wobbly but she was happy to be on solid ground again.

Jesse unlatched the metal door leading to the crypt. Suzy led Ali down the ramp through the entrance. It was cold and dark inside. The horse whinnied as his hooves touched the cool soft earth near the entrance of the underground chamber. As they continued inside, the earth was covered with floorboards which creaked underneath the horse's weight. The sound echoed and bounced off the stone walls.

Underneath the archway, three large stone coffins rested in the center of the crypt.

"I guess those are the three dead bishops that Julian mentioned," said Jesse. "Why are they buried down here?"

"This place is awfully creepy," said Suzy. The horse

nuzzled against her arm. "Look Jess, I think Ali knows we're trying to rescue him. Isn't he smart?"

"I hope he's smart enough to find himself a good hiding place down here."

There weren't any hiding places. As the girls guided the horse around the crypt, they noticed several doors but they were all locked. The center of the crypt was empty, except for the three dead bishops.

"Maybe we could hitch Whatshisface to one of those coffins?" asked Jesse.

"No, his reins aren't long enough," said Jesse. "Besides, it's probably a sin or something. But there's got to be someplace safe for Ali down here."

In the corner of the crypt a large wooden door swung open and Greg Wyatt, the sculptor, emerged. His sudden appearance took the horse by surprise. Ali reared up on his hind legs and whinnied nervously. The frightening cry echoed loudly through the chamber.

Greg was just as startled as the horse. "What on earth—is that a *horse*?" He stared at the girls on either side of AliFarabi. "Is this *your* horse?"

"Not exactly," Suzy admitted.

"What are you kids doing down here?" asked Greg. "What's going on?"

Suzy patted Ali to calm him down. "We need help. This is a horse in distress. If you love animals you'll help us find him a safe place. His name is AliFarabi."

"Please hide him somewhere," said Jesse. "It's just for a little while until we can reach his owner."

Greg approached the horse cautiously. "Who is his owner?" he asked.

"We don't know," Jesse admitted.

"Ali has to be at the National Horse Show tonight," said Suzy. "He's competing. He's a *champion.*"

Greg stroked Ali's flank. "Yes, I can see this horse is valuable. He's a beautiful animal. But if he's not yours, what are you doing with him? And why did you bring him down here?"

"We had to protect him," said Jesse. "Shiny Shoes was going to slit his ankles."

"Who's Shiny Shoes?" asked Greg.

"He's a horrible criminal," said Suzy. "He doesn't want Ali to win tonight so he stole him away from his stable. We found out about it so we stole Ali away from him."

"We *rescued* him," Jesse corrected.

"From a fate worse than death," Suzy added.

Greg looked puzzled as he stroked Ali's mane. "I don't understand this. You'd better come in my studio and explain it all."

"We just explained it," said Jesse.

"Then explain it *again,*" said Greg, unlocking his door.

As the door swung open, the girls stared inside Greg Wyatt's studio. It was huge. The ceiling inside was almost as high as the one in the crypt. There was an upper loft area filled with unfinished sculpture and books. A large table was stacked with plaster casts of animals. A long work table was filled with clay structures covered with moist rags. Everything smelled of wet clay and sawdust.

In one corner, Suzy noticed an unfinished sculpture of a lion almost ten feet high. "You sure build big things," she said admiringly. "How do you do it?"

"Never mind about me," said Greg, "let's hear about you girls and this horse,"

AliFarabi pawed the ground impatiently and tugged on his reins.

"Maybe he doesn't like the smell in here," said Jesse.

"Maybe he's hungry," said Suzy.

"Maybe he'd like some carrots," Greg suggested. "I keep a bag in the desk for the rabbits in the garden." He removed the carrots and gave them to Suzy. "Okay now, give me the facts. I can see this horse is valuable. But how did you discover this plot? And how did you meet this crook, Shiny Shoes? I can't help you unless you tell me everything."

Suzy fed Ali the carrots and began telling Greg their story. As Jesse listened, she quickly realized Suzy wasn't telling the *whole* story. Suzy made sure she never mentioned Calvin or Sarabeth.

Suzy finished the explanation at the same time Ali finished the carrots. "That's it," she concluded, "that's why it's vital we return Ali before the horse show tonight."

Greg scratched his head. "I still don't know how you girls figured all this out, but I believe you. I'm calling the police."

"Do you have to call in the police?" asked Suzy nervously.

"Of course. They'll find this man, Shiny Shoes. Maybe he's still following you."

"Don't worry, we shook him," said Jesse proudly. "Besides, we don't even know his name."

"The police will investigate all that," said Greg. "I don't have a phone down here so I'll have to use the one in the Dean's office. But don't worry, you'll be safe until I get back. My studio door locks automatically, so you can hide here just in case this person Shiny Shoes is hanging around somewhere."

84

"I told you, we shook him," said Jesse. "He'll never find us down here."

"That's good," said Greg, "but don't take chances. Stay here and look after AliFarabi until I get back. And promise you won't open the door for anyone."

"We promise," said Jesse. "Thanks."

As Greg left, the heavy wooden door of his studio slammed shut behind him.

"What a nice man," said Jesse.

Suzy ran to the door and pressed her ear against it. "I think he's gone. C'mon, now we can leave."

"What for? Why should we leave?" asked Jesse.

"You heard him, he's calling the *police.*"

"So what?"

"So we can't stay here and wait for the police. They'll ask us our names and then we'll have to reveal our identities. Then they'll start roasting us for information until . . ."

"You mean grilling."

". . . until we're forced to tell about our crooked siblings. And I refuse to tell the police about Sarabeth."

"She's a horsenapper," Jesse argued, "and so is Calvin. The two of them are in this up to their eyeballs. They were the front for Shiny Shoes. They pretended Alibaba was Sebastian. They made phony arrangements to board Sebastian in the city when they really planned to switch horses."

"I don't care," said Suzy. "Maybe what Sarabeth did was awful but I won't snitch on her."

"I'll gladly snitch on Calvin. I want to see him get what's coming to him."

"Do you really want to be responsible for his going to jail?" asked Suzy. "The police will probably find out the truth anyway without our help."

Jesse thought about that. Calvin could be really

spiteful. He still hadn't forgiven her for the time she'd deliberately thrown his favorite wool sweater in the washing machine while it was on the hot cycle. Although the sweater shrunk to nothing Calvin kept it—and he kept threatening to shove it down Jesse's throat someday. What vile thing would he do if he learned she'd fingered him? When Calvin got out of prison he'd probably *kill* her! "Maybe you're right," she agreed. "We'll let the cops handle this. Let's get out of here!"

Suzy stroked Ali's mane. "I hate to leave you alone but you'll be safe down here," she said lovingly. She tied his reins around the work table and gave him a final pat. "Okay, let's go."

As the girls left the studio, the door locked shut behind them. They hurried toward the entrance of the crypt, then climbed the stairs. Outside, the grounds around the Cathedral were quiet. It was Saturday, so the school children weren't around, the recycling center wasn't open, and the stonemasons weren't at work. They tiptoed around the side entrance of the Cathedral. The last tour bus had left for the day and it was empty inside. Suzy climbed the steps.

"Hold it, where are you going?" asked Jesse.

"This'll only take a minute," said Suzy. Ever since the Feast of St. Francis, Suzy felt the inside of the Cathedral was a miraculous place. When she'd seen that horse come down the aisle, she'd imagined herself there with Sebastian. Having Sebastian blessed had been a special moment and she wanted the same protection for Ali. "I'd like to pray for Ali to be reunited with his owner in time for the show."

"Okay, but hurry. We can't be around when the cops arrive."

It was cool and dark inside the Cathedral. The girls could hear their shoes click against the marble floors. They slipped into a pew and knelt down.

As Suzy glanced toward the stained glass rose window, she said a short prayer that everything would turn out all right. She prayed Ali would be safe, Shiny Shoes would be caught, and Sarabeth would abandon her sordid life of crime.

Jesse said a quick prayer, too. "Please straighten Calvin out," she asked. "He's a lousy brother but he's the only one I've got."

Suddenly the stillness in the church was interrupted. The girls heard footsteps coming down the aisle, then someone slipped into the pew behind them. Suddenly, each of them was grabbed by the back of the neck by a strong, clammy hand. They turned around and saw Shiny Shoes!

He leered at them menacingly. "What's wrong, aren't you glad to see me?" He linked their arms together, then twisted them behind their backs. "What'd you do with the horsey?"

"We won't tell you," gasped Suzy.

Shiny Shoes tightened his grip. "What'd you do with him?" he repeated.

"You can't scare us," said Suzy.

"You'd better tell me," he threatened. "Or do you want me to break your arms first?"

"You're bluffing," said Jesse. "We're the only ones who know where Aliwhatsit is. You won't hurt us."

"You think so? The way I figure, you two are the only ones to snitch on me. A charge of attempted grand theft would put me back in jail so long they'd throw away the key."

"We're not the only ones who know about you," said Suzy.

"Those teenagers? They'll keep their mouths shut, they're accomplices. But I can't take chances with you kids blabbing what you know."

"We're your *insurance,* you said so yourself," said Jesse.

"That was earlier," said Shiny Shoes. "Now I'm taking out a new policy. Give me that horsey or you're both gonna get it."

"We won't," said Suzy.

"Relax, I won't hurt him," Shiny Shoes assured her. "I just want to get him back to Meadowbrook so no one's the wiser. Without evidence there's no crime, right? And you've got the evidence." He loosened his grip and removed his pocketknife. "But if you won't cooperate, this has a blade for everything, know what I mean?"

Suzy figured the truth was as good as anything they could make up. "We *can't* give you the horse. He's in a locked studio in the crypt, and we don't have the key."

"No problem," Shiny Shoes responded with a sneer. "I've picked a few locks in my time. Now, be good little girls and show me where that horse is."

"That's not a good idea," Suzy said, feeling very brave. "It's Greg's studio and he went to call the police. They'll probably be there before you could pick the lock and get away. You'd better just forget about AliFarabi and get out of here fast."

Shiny Shoes seemed to be thinking about what Suzy had said, as if he believed her and was trying to figure out what to do. Finally he spoke. "Okay, but I'm not going to leave the two of you here to tell the cops about our little conversation. If I'm leaving, you're leaving with me."

Suddenly Suzy didn't feel quite so brave. Why

hadn't she realized how dangerous she and Jesse were to Shiny Shoes now that he'd practically confessed to them that he'd stolen AliFarabi? And why was Jesse, who usually had something to say about everything, being so quiet? She could hear her in the pew next to her, messing around with a pile of missal books. Jesse sure picked a funny time to get interested in reading, Suzy thought.

It happened so quickly Suzy didn't realize at first what was going on. Shiny Shoes reached to grab her, and at the same moment Jesse threw the missal books into Shiny Shoe's face. He stumbled and fell. Then Jesse and Suzy scrambled out of the pew.

They knew Shiny Shoes would be caught off guard only for a few seconds—not enough time for them to run down the long aisle and escape through the main doors. So they did the next best thing. Crawling on their hands and knees, they hid behind a pew on the opposite aisle. There, near the side wall, Jesse noticed a small oak door, partially open. "Let's make our getaway through there," she whispered. They crept toward the door, slowly slid through it, then tiptoed up a flight of stairs.

They had reached the Cathedral's second level. There, a narrow gallery called the triforium ran along the south side, just below the clerestory windows. It had been turned into makeshift office space, filled with desks and messy bookshelves. From this arcade, the stained glass windows seemed close enough to reach out and touch.

Jesse peeked over the edge of the gallery. She could see Shiny Shoes on the first level, forty feet below. He was still looking for them, inspecting every pew.

"We're in luck, he didn't see us come up here," she whispered.

"Let's hide somewhere just in case," said Suzy.

The girls crawled underneath a desk and tried to stay quiet, almost afraid to breathe. Below the gallery, they could hear Shiny Shoes scurrying around in the aisles inspecting every corner. His leather heels squeaked along the marble and echoed up through the triforium.

"He's going to find us pretty soon," gasped Suzy. "We're sitting ducks up here."

Jesse glanced around. In the corner a few feet away, she saw a darkened alcove with two steps leading toward a small door. "Maybe that's an exit. Let's try it."

"What if it's not an exit?" asked Suzy nervously. "What if it's a closet or something? We'll be stuck there like rats in a trap!"

As Suzy fidgeted underneath the desk, she knocked one of the books to the ground. It slipped through the gallery opening and dropped to the floor of the church below.

Shiny Shoes heard the noise and looked up. "So that's where you creeps are!" he shouted. He glanced around, saw the small oak door, and hurried toward it.

"We'll have to try that door," said Jesse. "It's our only escape." She quickly crawled out from underneath the desk and Suzy followed. The girls ran toward the door, lifted the heavy iron latch and pushed it open. The escape route they had hoped for didn't exist. Behind the door lay only darkness.

Suzy banged against the wall. "I told you, it's a *closet.* We're trapped!"

Jesse tried not to panic. As she fumbled around in the blackness, she tripped over a narrow stone step. "No, Suz, it's a stairway. The stairs are real skinny and they go around."

"A circular staircase? Where does it lead?"

"It's too dark to see. We'll have to climb up and find out."

"Do you think Shiny Shoes knows we came in here?"

"He'll probably take a while to find the door," said Jesse. "By then, we'll have escaped."

"We can't escape by climbing *up*," Suzy argued.

"Well, we can't go back down," said Jesse.

As the girls climbed the narrow circular stairs, they moved through total darkness. The stairs wound further and further upward, always leading to more stairs.

"Hold it, I need to catch my breath," said Suzy.

Below them, the heavy metal door swung open, then closed. The sound of it reverberated ominously throughout the stone stairway.

"Keep moving," said Jesse. "Shiny Shoes is on his way!"

No light penetrated the narrow space and the girls felt helpless trapped in the dark. The higher they climbed, the darker it became, like an ever-ascending tunnel of blackness.

Jesse's heart was beating like a hammer and her legs were aching. "This has to end pretty soon."

Down below, Shiny Shoes was wheezing and puffing, trying hard to catch up.

Then, suddenly, the steps stopped. They had finally reached the end of their destination but it didn't lead anywhere.

"Some crazy person built a staircase leading *nowhere!*" Suzy shouted.

Jesse ran her fingers along the wall. "I feel something. I think it's a doorknob."

As she turned the knob and pushed open the door, sunlight spilled into the narrow space. For a second it was so bright, it almost blinded Jesse. "Where are we?" She stepped outside. A wide ledge extended along the South Front of the Cathedral, high above the ground. "We must've climbed the stairs Julian told us about."

As Suzy followed, a sudden chill wind whipped around the stone statuary suspended from the Cathedral's face. "It's awfully windy up here." Her knees trembled. "This is awful. Now we're really trapped. How can we escape from up here? We're sitting ducks!"

"Stop saying that!" Jesse shouted. "This mess is all your fault. If you hadn't gone into the church to say a prayer, we never would've . . ."

"Don't blame me for everything. Let's figure out what to do. How do we keep Shiny Shoes from getting us?"

Jesse glanced around the roof. "Maybe we can find some loose stones to push against the door."

"That might work," said Suzy. "Or maybe we could . . ."

Suzy and Jesse froze in their tracks as they heard the door suddenly swing open. Shiny Shoes was standing in the entrance. "Okay, kids, the game is over," he said, panting.

The girls ran to the rim of the ledge.

"You can't escape." Shiny Shoes flashed an evil smile as he approached. "I couldn't have planned this better. You're making my job real easy."

"Don't touch us!" Jesse shouted. She climbed onto the ledge and stared down into the stoneyard below. It seemed so far away. Just looking down at it made her dizzy.

"Don't come any closer or we'll scream our heads off!" Suzy threatened, climbing up beside Jesse.

Shiny Shoes came closer. "You kids aren't as smart as you think. I figured how this whole deal can work in my favor. *You kids* stole that horse from the stable. *You kids* hid it somewhere. So, *you kids* will be blamed for everything. That's how the cops will see it. Then you kids climbed up here to escape and you fell off the roof. Isn't that a shame?"

"You can't kill us," Suzy gasped. "The police will find out the truth. They're on their way and they'll be here any minute."

"Who are you kidding? Anyway, the cops have nothing on me. You kids'll get blamed for this whole mess." Shiny Shoes moved closer. "One push and it's all over."

"They'll find out and get you!" Jesse shouted.

Shiny Shoes laughed. "Me? I'm not here. How can I be blamed if two crazy kids fall off the roof?"

Suzy desperately clung to the ledge. "This is awful, Jess, what'll we do?"

Jesse stared down toward the Cathedral grounds. In the distance, she caught a glimpse of Greg Wyatt's Peace Fountain. She saw the wings of St. Michael, the avenging angel. Maybe *he* could help. "Close your eyes and pray for a *miracle.*"

"I'm too scared to close my eyes and I think it's too late to pray!"

"Then stop complaining," Jesse snapped. "Isn't it bad enough we're going to die?"

"SOMEONE HELP US!" Suzy screamed. The wind seemed to swallow up her words.

Shiny Shoes reached out to grab their feet. Frantically, the girls inched their way toward the far end of the ledge, just out of his reach.

Suzy knew they were going to die. It wasn't fair but there wasn't anything to do about it. She squeezed Jesse's hand. "I'm sorry I whined so much. I guess I never should've tried to rescue Ali."

Suddenly, a loud voice floated up toward the top of the Cathedral. "Are you kids okay?"

Jesse and Suzy looked down. It was Greg Wyatt! With him were two policemen and a security guard.

"Help, Shiny Shoes is trying to kill us!" Jesse wailed.

Shiny Shoes backed away. "I'm getting out of here," he said, running to the door.

"He's coming down," Suzy shouted.

"Guard the exits," Jesse ordered. "Don't let him escape!"

"Don't worry, we'll catch him," the policeman yelled up.

"Hang on, I'm coming to get you," Greg shouted.

"We're saved," said Jesse. "It's a miracle!"

"Are you girls all right?" asked the security guard as Jesse and Suzy sat on the bench outside the garden.

"Sure, we're okay," said Jesse.

"Why did you go up to the roof?" asked Greg. "You promised me you'd wait in the crypt."

"That was all my fault," Suzy admitted.

The two policemen came by with Shiny Shoes. "This guy won't admit anything," said Officer Martinez. "He insists he's innocent."

"But he tried to *kill* us!" said Jesse.

"Mr. Monroe says he was trying to *rescue* you," explained Officer Grady. "He says he passed by and saw you kids hanging off the roof."

"Mr. Monroe is a filthy *liar!*" said Suzy.

"What were you two doing up there?" asked Officer Martinez suspiciously.

"We can't book Mr. Monroe on assault charges

without some evidence," explained Officer Grady. "Are you girls sure you're telling us everything?"

Jesse and Suzy were silent.

"Maybe they're frightened," Greg suggested. "The girls told me this man was following them. They said he'd stolen a valuable horse which I allowed them to bring into my studio."

"Those rotten kids are lying," Shiny Shoes insisted. "I'm innocent. I was doing a good deed. I only went up to the roof to help them. And I don't know anything about a horse. I wouldn't know a champion racehorse from a milk horse."

"We have evidence against you," said Jesse. "The woman in the office at Claremont Stables will identify you."

"So what? I've a right to visit a stable if I like. That's no proof I stole anything. *You* did it."

"We didn't steal Ali, we *rescued* him," Suzy argued.

Officer Grady looked confused. "Was everyone trying to *rescue* someone? Are you sure there's been a crime committed here?"

"Of course there's a crime," said Jesse. "It's grand larceny."

"I'm not involved, honest," said Shiny Shoes. "Those two teenagers did it."

"What teenagers?" asked Officer Grady.

Shiny Shoes stared at Jesse and Suzy. "Ask *them*, they're all in it together."

Officer Grady stared at Jesse and Suzy. "What teenagers?"

Jesse stared at Suzy. "I guess it's no use."

Suzy sighed. "You're right, we'll have to tell *everything*."

Chapter Fifteen

The police car cut through traffic, its emergency siren blasting. Shiny Shoes sat in the backseat with Officer Grady. Jesse and Suzy sat up front with Officer Martinez.

"I keep telling you guys I'm innocent," Shiny Shoes protested.

"Don't worry, Mr. Monroe, we'll get to the truth real soon," Officer Grady assured him.

Suzy felt awful. She hated to squeal on Sarabeth but she had no choice. Now that the police were involved, the truth had to come out.

Jesse's feelings were mixed. She didn't mind snitching on Calvin but what would he do for revenge?

The police car screeched to a halt outside the Claremont Academy. When the girls got out, they saw Calvin and Sarabeth. Then they saw two more policemen plus their *parents*.

Jesse cringed. "What're our parents doing here?"

Mr. and Mrs. Leroy and Mr. and Mrs. Pierce all began talking at once.

"Jess, explain all this," Mr. Leroy insisted.

"Why'd you do it?" asked Mrs. Leroy.

"Suzanne, I hope there's a good reason for this trouble," said Mrs. Pierce.

"Why'd you steal that horse?" asked Mr. Pierce.

"I didn't steal anything," Suzy protested. "I tried to keep Sarabeth from stealing."

"That's a disgusting lie!" Sarabeth shouted.

"They're both little creeps," said Calvin.

Officer Grady and Officer Martinez introduced themselves to Officer Freidrich and Officer Krump.

"Someone from Claremont called us," explained Officer Krump.

"Someone at the Cathedral called us," said Officer Grady.

They began filling one another in on the details. But the four policemen couldn't unravel the confusion.

The girls were confused, too. "What are Mom and Dad doing here?" asked Suzy.

"I called them," said Sarabeth. "When you galloped off on Sebastian, nice Mr. Monroe tried catching up with you. I knew you must've gone crazy."

"You're the one who's crazy," said Suzy. "Mr. Monroe isn't nice at all."

"And that horse isn't Sebastian," Jesse added.

"Of course it is," said Sarabeth. "What did you do with him?"

"The horse is safe in the Cathedral complex," said Officer Grady. "Now we have to find out who owns him."

"Mr. Bronson at Meadowbrook Stables owns Sebastian," said Sarabeth.

"We've leased the horse from Mr. Bronson," explained Mr. Pierce. "We plan to board him here at Claremont for a month so Suzanne can ride him."

"It's her surprise birthday present," added Mrs. Pierce.

Suzy was stunned. "Really? I thought you'd forgotten my birthday."

"We never forget your birthday," said Mrs. Pierce.

"But we should have!" said Sarabeth. "After all my hard work, look at the mess you've made. And think of the money I could have saved Mom and Dad. Nice Mr. Monroe offered to transport Sebastian *free.*"

"Quit calling him nice," Jesse insisted.

"He was extremely helpful," Sarabeth continued. "He said he was picking up another horse in the city so he offered to give Sebastian a free ride. We could have saved a lot of money but you ruined the entire plan."

"Then you really didn't know that horse *wasn't* Sebastian?" asked Suzy.

"It *is* Sebastian," Sarabeth insisted. "I told you, I arranged to have Mr. Monroe transport him here."

"It isn't Sebastian," said Jesse.

Calvin nudged Jesse. "Listen up, okay? Sarsy knocked herself out on this deal. She wanted it to be a surprise for her creepy sister."

Suzy was thrilled. "Then you guys really didn't know what was going on!"

"Hold it, don't let them off the hook so easy," said Jesse.

"I believe them," said Suzy. "I forgot Sarabeth has never *seen* Sebastian. She's never been inside the Meadowbrook stable."

"Stables smell," said Sarabeth.

Officer Krump was getting impatient. "Does anyone know for sure who this missing horse is?"

"It's AliFarabi," said Suzy. "He's a champion Arabian stallion scheduled to perform at the National Horse Show tonight."

"Mr. Monroe switched horses to keep Ali out of the running," Jesse explained.

"You can't prove that," said Shiny Shoes.

"Call Ali's owner," Suzy suggested.

"Sure," said Jesse. "When his owner goes to Meadowbrook to transport him, he'll find out he's missing."

Mr. Pierce looked annoyed. "Then where's Sebastian? Since I'm paying for a month's board, I'd like to know where the animal is."

"He's probably still at Meadowbrook," said Suzy. "Don't you see, Dad? Mr. Monroe must've spotted Sarabeth for a dope right away. He saw she had no horse sense so he tricked her into thinking he was doing her a favor."

"You can't prove that," Shiny Shoes insisted.

"We'd better prove something soon," said Officer Krump.

Mr. Leroy looked confused. "What does Jesse have to do with all this?"

"The society was her idea," said Suzy.

"What society?" asked Mrs. Leroy.

"It's a secret so we can't tell you anything about it," said Jesse.

Mrs. Leroy eyed her suspiciously. "I should've known something was up when you went to the *library*."

"Yeah, you can't trust either of them," said Calvin. "They're stinking spies."

"I'm calling Meadowbrook right now," said Officer Krump.

"And I'm checking Monroe for priors," said Officer Martinez. "We need straight answers right away."

Inside the office of the Claremont Riding Academy, everyone sat waiting nervously. When Officers Martinez and Krump finished their phone calls, the truth began to unfold.

"Here's how it breaks down," said Officer Krump. "I called Mr. Bronson at Meadowbrook. He phoned Lowell Esterbrand, the owner of AliFarabi. Mr. Esterbrand just arrived at Meadowbrook. He says his horse isn't there. Which means the horse hidden in the crypt at St. John the Divine is probably his."

"Just like we told you," said Suzy.

"And I checked Monroe for priors," said Officer Martinez. "He's served time for bank robbery so maybe he's not so innocent."

"Just like we told you," said Jesse.

Officer Grady stared at Shiny Shoes. "Maybe you'd better come clean, Mr. Monroe."

"Hold it, I'm not taking this rap alone," shouted Shiny Shoes.

"Who was in it with you?" asked Officer Freidrich. "Give evidence and you might get time off."

"Okay. I was hired by Mr. Whitlaw, a rival owner with a horse in the show tonight. Whitlaw wanted to sabotage things. With Esterbrand's horse out of the running, he figured his horse would win big. He planned for me to switch horses up at Meadowbrook. When these teenagers came along asking to bring another horse to the city, I thought I had a perfect set-up . . . until those two kids screwed it up."

"Then these teenagers had nothing to do with the horsenapping?" asked Officer Krump.

"I duped them," Shiny Shoes admitted. "It was easy. But those two kids nearly drove me crazy."

"So you tried to *kill* us," shouted Jesse.

"I never would've done that," said Shiny Shoes. "I just wanted to scare you into giving me the horse."

"I think we've heard enough," said Officer Martinez.

"Thank goodness this mess is finally over," said Mr. Pierce.

On the walk home, Suzy felt like she was floating. Pretty soon she would have a whole month with Sebastian! She could ride him in Central Park every day after school and all day on weekends. It would be *heaven*. "Boarding Sebastian is the best present I've ever had," she said.

"Thank Sarabeth," said Mrs. Pierce. "It was her idea."

A heavy lump suddenly replaced Suzy's lightness. Sarabeth wasn't a horse thief but she was still an *art* thief. But how could she send her sister off to rot in jail? Sarabeth had been so thoughtful, how could Suzy turn her in?

Suzy's mind raced for a solution. Luckily, the police knew nothing about the stolen statue. Since Shiny Shoes wasn't involved, they had no clues.

Suzy made a solemn vow to take the secret to her grave. "Don't worry, Sarabeth," she whispered. "I'll never snitch on you. Promise to turn over a new leaf and I'll never tell."

"What are you babbling about?" asked Sarabeth.

"I think she's trying to save your skin," said Jesse. "We know about the other theft."

"We saw you switch those statues in the museum," Suzy explained. "Promise to get therapy and I'll never tell."

Jesse nudged Calvin. "I guess I won't tell on you either, musclehead."

Calvin shrugged. "There's nothing to tell, bird-brain."

Mr. and Mrs. Pierce stared at Mrs. and Mr. Leroy. "What are the children whispering about?" asked Mrs. Leroy.

Sarabeth laughed out loud. "Suzy, you're an incredible little jerk! I don't know why I wanted to do something nice for you. I guess I hoped it would turn you into a human being. I've never stolen anything, you idiot."

"Yes you did," Suzy protested. "We were there watching."

"Snooping, you mean," said Calvin.

"We *saw* you," Suzy insisted.

"I know," said Sarabeth smugly. "We saw you, too."

"We saw you see us," said Calvin. "We knew you were on our tail from the start."

"That's right," said Sarabeth. "We decided to teach you a lesson, make things more interesting."

"Heat up the chase," said Calvin.

"Make you *squirm,"* said Sarabeth.

"You're lying," said Jesse. "We were perfect snoops; you never saw us."

"You were lousy snoops," said Calvin, doubling over with laughter. "We found your sappy pact the day you worms wrote it. We knew what was up so we planned all that junk in Central Park."

"Why?" asked Jesse.

"We told you, to teach you worms a lesson, wart-face."

"I don't believe it," said Suzy. "Why'd you switch those statues in the museum?"

"That statue was to be a birthday present," Sarabeth explained. "Aunt Alberta sent Mom money for

102

your gift and I thought you should get something cultural."

"And I thought we should make it look like a caper," said Calvin proudly. "I let that note slip from my pocket so you'd find it."

"I argued with the salesgirl so you'd be suspicious," said Sarabeth.

Suzy still didn't believe it. "Why'd you snoop around in Chinatown? I saw you sneak into that restaurant."

"I was arranging your surprise birthday dinner," explained Sarabeth.

"I don't like Chinese food," said Suzy.

"I know, but *I* do," said Sarabeth. "So does anyone with any sense."

Calvin poked Jesse. "We rehearsed all those stupid phone calls, too. We knew you creeps listened in. Made you squirm, didn't we?"

"You've known all along we've been following you?" asked Jesse.

"Not quite," Sarabeth admitted. "We didn't know you'd trailed us today. I wanted Suzy's real present to stay a surprise. I never discussed the details on the phone. How'd you find out?"

"We dug your notes from the garbage," Suzy confessed.

Sarabeth sighed. "I might've known. You really are a cruddy little sister, you know it?"

Suzy hugged her. "You're a *wonderful* sister," she said. "It was your idea to bring me Sebastian. Thank you forever!"

Sarabeth hugged her back. "You're welcome. Maybe it was worth the bother. Anyway, happy birthday."

Everyone seemed very friendly by the time the group arrived home.

"I'm not sure what you kids were angry about," said Mr. Pierce, "but I'm glad you've settled it before dinner."

"Which is going to be a surprise," added Mrs. Pierce. "In honor of Suzy's birthday, we'd like you all to join us at . . ."

"Ming-Sum-Loo's Restaurant in Chinatown," said Suzy.

"How did you know that?" asked Mr. Pierce.

"Let's face it, Dad," said Sarabeth. "You can't hide things from Suzy. She's a super snoop."

Chapter Sixteen

The opening night of the National Horse Show was spectacular. Famous trainers, riders, and former members of the Olympic Equestrian Team were there. Suzy recognized lots of them, and before the show she got their autographs.

"This is more fun than the circus!" said Jesse.

Suzy admired all the horses. She loved the matched bays ridden by the Royal Canadian Mounted Police. She loved watching the Mounties assemble in their scarlet tunics before parading their horses through the arena. And she loved all the exhibitions of ringcraft that followed.

Mr. Pierce checked the program. "AliFarabi is up next. He's riding in the Combined Training Class. He'll be performing dressage, cross country, and stadium jumping."

"That's the hardest class," Suzy told Jesse. "Only the best horses make it because they have to do *everything.*"

Suzy watched as Ali's rider, Jim Spence, entered the ring and began dressage movements. As Jim put him through his paces, Ali obeyed each command perfectly. As Suzy watched, she was sure she saw Ali glance her way. As Ali raised his front legs high into the air it looked as if he gave her a *wink*.

"Ali is the best horse ever," said Suzy.

"What about Sebastian?" asked Jesse.

"Okay, Ali is second best," said Suzy.

After the show everyone went back to congratulate Jim Spence, Ali's handler, Mr. Brent, and Mr. Esterbrand, Ali's owner.

Lowell Esterbrand was thrilled to meet them. "So these are the two girls who rescued my champion."

"That's us," said Jesse proudly.

"We were glad to do it," said Suzy. "I bet Ali wins first prize."

"I'm sure he will," said Mr. Esterbrand excitedly. "He scored well tonight. He ran in record time and he had no faults. But AliFarabi wouldn't be here tonight if it weren't for you girls. How can I repay you? The police didn't explain how you uncovered the plot."

"Luckily, our daughters were in the right place at the right time," said Mr. Leroy.

"Arrangements were being made at Meadowbrook for us to lease a horse for Suzy and board it in the city," Mrs. Pierce explained.

"I see," said Mr. Esterbrand. "Then please allow me to pay your year's boarding and leasing fees."

"A *year*?" gasped Suzy.

"We only planned to lease Sebastian for a month," Mr. Pierce explained.

"A month? That's nothing," said Mr. Esterbrand. "I know how young girls love horses."

"I don't love horses," said Jesse. "I don't even know how to ride."

"Then allow me to add a year's free riding lessons

106

for you, young lady. And I won't take no for an answer."

"What a great idea," said Suzy. "Pretty soon, *both* of us will be champion horsewomen."

"That's a very generous offer," said Mr. Leroy.

"Yes, thank you," said Mr. Pierce.

"I can hardly wait to see Sebastian," said Suzy. "When does he arrive at Claremont?"

"He's due on Monday," said Mrs. Pierce.

Suzy was delighted. "Didn't everything work out just great, Jess? It's almost like a miracle."

"You'd better pray for another one," Jesse groaned. "That rotten book report is also due on Monday!"

Jesse squirmed in her seat as Mr. MacPherson finished reading aloud her book report.

. . . So I never read the book about Quasimodo. But I saw the movie twice. I never rang the giant bells like Quasimodo did, but I know what it's like to hang off the side of a cathedral. And I know a cathedral can be a sanctuary for people— and for horses, too. I'm glad there's still a real cathedral like the ones they built hundreds of years ago. Even though I never read the book, I know how the Hunchback of Notre Dame must have felt.

Mr. MacPherson cleared his throat. "As a book report this is a failure. But as a composition it's a success."

"I don't suppose that means I passed?" asked Jesse hopefully.

"Yes it does," said Mr. MacPherson. "As long as you read the book by the end of the term."

"I will, I promise," Jesse vowed.

She had actually passed English. That *was* a miracle!

"So what do you think of him?" asked Suzy proudly. Dressed in her livery, Suzy escorted Sebastian down the heated ramp of Claremont Stables.

Jesse stroked his shiny brown mane. "He's okay, I guess."

Sebastian flared his nostrils, stamped his feet, and whinnied happily.

"He likes you," said Suzy. "Here, give him a carrot." Cautiously, Jesse fed Sebastian. His tongue tickled the palm of her hand and he made slobbery sounds as he crunched. "Yeah, he's really okay," said Jesse.

"Maybe next year, Sebastian will be chosen to be in the Feast of St. Francis," said Suzy hopefully. "And maybe he can join the Snoop Society, too."

"He can take my place," said Jesse. "I never want to snoop on Calvin and Sarabeth again. I don't care what they do together!"

"Now that we're *professionals,* it might be fun to snoop on something else. Do you think anything else interesting will turn up?"

Jesse laughed. "Are you kidding? This is New York City, Suz. There's always something interesting happening here."

"That's right," Suzy agreed, "there always is!"